S
A
POEMS   I
OF A   G
MOUNTAIN   Y
HOME   Ō

Translations from the
Oriental Classics

SAIGYŌ

POEMS
OF A
MOUNTAIN
HOME

TRANSLATED BY
BURTON WATSON

New York
Columbia University Press

Columbia University Press
New York   Oxford

Copyright © 1991 Columbia University Press
All rights reserved

Library of Congress Cataloging-in-Publication Data
Saigyō, 1118–1190.
  [Sankashū. English]
  Saigyō, poems of a mountain home / translated by Burton Watson.
    p.   cm.
  Translations from the oriental classics. Cf. Added t.p.
  ISBN 0-231-07492-1
    1. Saigyō, 1118–1190—Translations, English.   2. Waka—
Translations into English.   3. Waka, English—Translations from
Japanese.   I. Watson, Burton, 1925–   II. Title.   III. Title:
Poems of a mountain home.
PL788.5.S213   1991
895.6'114—dc20   90-32449
                                                  CIP

⬥

Printed in the United States of America
c 10 9 8 7 6 5 4 3 2 1

Translations
from the
Oriental Classics

EDITORIAL BOARD
Wm. Theodore de Bary, Chairman

C. T. Hsia
Donald Keene
Barbara Stoler Miller
Burton Watson
Philip B. Yampolsky

CONTENTS

1
Introduction

17
Spring

53
Summer

65
Autumn

85
Winter

103
Love

121
Miscellaneous

221
Poems from the *Kikigaki shū*

POEMS
OF A
MOUNTAIN
HOME

S
A
I
G
Y
Ō

I
N
T
R
O
D
U
C
T
I
O
N

SAIGYŌ—for a Japanese reader, the name evokes images of thatched-roofed retreats in isolated mountain settings, of a solitary traveler over distant roads, a Buddhist poet-priest who in his works celebrated both the beauty and the evanescence of the·phenomenal world, and was not ashamed to confess his unending passion for blossoming cherries and the moon in the night sky Though relatively little is known about his life— the popularly held image of him is strongly colored by later legend—there can be little doubt of his importance as a poet. He is the leading figure in the famous anthology entitled *Shinkokinshū* or "New Collection of Ancient and Modern Times," being represented by a total of ninety-four poems, while his collected works, the *Sankashū* or "Mountain Home Collection," preserves some fifteen hundred poems from his hand. Because of the originality that marks his best works, their simplicity, directness, and air of somber beauty, he has come to rank as one of the most influential figures of the Japanese court poetry tradition.

Saigyō started out in life under the name Satō Norikiyo, the son of a well-to-do warrior family that was a branch of the eminent Fujiwara clan. He was born in 1118 in Kyoto, the capital of Heian period Japan, where his father held a military post. As a young man he received training in the martial arts and became a retainer to the Tokudaiji family, another branch of the Fujiwara clan. The Tokudaijis at this time boasted several male members in high ministerial posts in the imperial government and a daughter, known as Taikemmon-in, who was consort to Emperor Toba (r. 1107–1123) and mother of emperors Sutoku (r. 1123–1141) and Go-Shirakawa (r. 1155–1158). Through his connections with the Tokudaiji family, Norikiyo was able in time to become a member of the *hokumen-no-bushi*, the elite private guard of Emperor Toba, who by this time had abdicated and was living in retirement.

In 1140, when Norikiyo was no more than twenty-two—twenty-three by Japanese reckoning, which counts a person as one year old at birth—he abruptly quit this post to enter religious life as a Buddhist priest. Various reasons have been suggested for the action: an unhappy love affair, possibly with a woman far above him in social station; shock at the sudden death of a family member or members; disillusionment with the seamier aspects of aristocratic life; or general unease over the far-reaching social changes of the period. All such suggestions are mere guesswork. The only thing certain is that, for someone of his youth and affluent background, the step was an unusual one. He may at the time have had a wife, and perhaps even children, though nothing is known for sure.

By the closing years of the Heian period, when Saigyō lived, the system of imperial rule was functioning very imperfectly. The great Fujiwara clan, which had earlier dominated the government, was beginning to wane in influence, and the emperors were attempting to exercise their right to rule as they had in previous times, often by abdicating at an early age and then wielding authority from behind the scenes in a manner known as *insei* or "government by cloistered emperor." But increasingly the truly decisive power in political affairs was passing into the hands of the warrior clans that had grown up in the provinces, particularly the Minamoto clan, with its base in northeastern Japan, and the Taira clan, whose lands and influence lay in the central and western provinces.

In 1156, when a dispute over succession to the throne known as the Hōgen disturbance broke out in the capital, warriors of both the Minamoto and Taira clans became involved in the fighting. In 1159, a second outbreak of hostilities in the capital found the two clans confronting each other as competitors for dominance. The Taira emerged victorious, and for the following twenty years their leader, Taira Kiyomori, conducted himself as virtual dictator of the nation. But by the time of his death in 1181, the Minamotos were once more openly challenging the rule of their rivals. Eventually they drove the Taira forces from the capital and hounded them to final defeat at the sea battle of Dannoura in 1185. Establishing a shogunate or military government at Kamakura in the east, they initiated a new system of warrior rule, an event that marks the close of the Heian and the beginning of the Kamakura period.

To many Japanese, particularly those like Saigyō who were closely allied with courtier circles in Kyoto, these cataclysmic social upheavals seemed to spell the demise of all that was worthwhile in their nation's culture and filled them with foreboding. In addition, there was another important factor that inclined the people of the time to a pessimistic outlook. According to Buddhist belief, after a Buddha dies—Shakyamuni Buddha, in the case of our present universe—although his teachings may prosper for some hundreds of years, they are destined in time to become debilitated by growing formalism and an ebbing of the tide of true faith. Eventually, in a period known as Mappō or the End of the Law, they will lose all power to guide human beings to enlightenment. When that happens, many people asserted, the only hope of salvation will lie in a savior known as Amida Buddha. For Amida has vowed to enable all those who have faith in him to be reborn in his Pure Land or Western Paradise, where enlightenment will be easy to attain. According to the reckonings of Japanese Buddhists, the fateful period of Mappō had already begun in 1052, over half a century before Saigyō's birth. The social chaos of the time, it was claimed, merely confirmed the fact that the world had entered an era of moral and spiritual decay.

Viewed against the background of these beliefs and historical events, Saigyō's abrupt abandonment of secular life becomes somewhat less surprising. In the later years of the Heian period a number of persons, usually members of the lower aristocracy or bureaucrats, embittered by the inequalities of class difference or frustrated in their careers, withdrew from society, in some instances to devote themselves to aesthetic pursuits or pure hedonism, but more often to take up some form of religious life. Already in the *Tale of Genji*, a work of the early eleventh century, we see the ideal of the eremitic life taking shape, a life that customarily combined literary and artistic interests and a keen sensitivity to the beauties of nature with the practice of Buddhist devotions and austerities.

In Saigyō's case, his main aim in quitting secular life, at least initially, may simply have been to create for himself an atmosphere of quiet in which his poetic talents could mature and flourish most effectively. We know that he was greatly influenced by earlier monk-poets such as Nōin (998–1050), or contemporary literary figures who lived in seclusion, and seems at an early age to have conceived a desire to imitate their example, though whether it was the religious aspect of their activities that appealed to him or the aesthetic, we cannot say. In the lives of such persons, aesthetic and religious concerns existed side by side, and it is perhaps unrealistic to attempt to draw too sharp a line between the two.

After becoming a monk, Saigyō at first went by the religious name En'i, but eventually settled on Saigyō, which means "Western Journey" and presumably derives from beliefs relating to Amida's Western Paradise. At this time such beliefs had not yet led to the establishment of any distinct sect or sects of Buddhism, as they were to do later, but flourished in the traditional centers of Tendai and Shingon Buddhism such as Mount Hiei and Mount Kōya, or at older temples like the Shitennō-ji in the area of present-day Osaka City.

For the first few years of his new life, Saigyō resided in mountain areas close to the capital such as Higashiyama, Kurama, and Saga that were favored spots for reclusion, sometimes in temples but more often, it would appear, in small huts or retreats of his own. Judging from his poems, he experienced considerable difficulty in tearing himself away from his friends and connections in the capital. Later, when he had presumably become better adjusted to the monastic calling, he lived much of his time on Mount Kōya, the headquarters of the Shingon sect with which he was affiliated, or on nearby Mount Yoshino, famous for its flowering cherries.

During these years he continued to devote much time to the writing of poetry, taking part in poetry contests at temples and shrines, visiting and exchanging poems with recluse friends, and keeping in close touch with poetry circles in the capital.

Such assiduous attention to literary pursuits on the part of a man who had supposedly dedicated himself to religion was eyed askance in some quarters. According to an anecdote recorded in a work entitled *Seiashō* by the poet Ton'a (1289–1372), Mongaku, an eminent Shingon priest who headed the Jingo-ji temple in the environs of Kyoto, though he had never met Saigyō, expressed strong disapproval of Saigyō's "aesthetic activities" (*suki*), observing that if one became a monk in the Buddhist Order he should devote himself solely to religious matters. Mongaku added that if he ever happened to encounter Saigyō, he intended to "split his head in two!" In time, the passage relates, Saigyō appeared at Mongaku's temple requesting permission to participate in a religious ceremony. Mongaku, far from splitting Saigyō's head in two, received him with great courtesy, evidently won over by the sincerity of Saigyō's manner.

Unfortunately, we have no way of knowing just how Saigyō himself viewed his poetic activities, whether he saw them as conflicting with, or supplementing, his religious strivings. One has the impression, however, that, particularly in his younger days, Saigyō had greater confidence in himself as a poet than as a practitioner of the Buddhist Law. [1]

As will be evident from the poems in the selection that follows, Saigyō made a number of trips around the country to visit shrines and temples or places famed for their scenic beauty. Two of his longest journeys were to the Michinoku region of far northern Honshu, which he visited once in his late twenties and again when he was nearing seventy. His paternal grandfather had been a member of the illustrious branch of the Fujiwara family that dominated that area, and

---

1. There are anecdotes such as that describing Saigyō's meeting with the priest Myōe (1173–1232) at Takao or with the priest Jien (1155–1225) at Mount Hiei that suggest he regarded the writing of poetry in Japanese as an act of religious devotion or an expression of Buddhist enlightenment. But these anecdotes appear in works compiled many decades after Saigyō's death and it is difficult to accept them as proof of his attitude toward poetry. For a fuller discussion of the relationship between poetry and religious practice in Saigyō's life, see Herbert Eugen Plutschow, "Japanese Travel Diaries of the Middle Ages," *Oriens Extremus* (1982), 29: 1–136, especially pp. 73–83, and Mezaki Tokue, "Aesthete-Recluses during the Transition from Ancient to Medieval Japan" in *Principles of Classical Japanese Literature*, Earl Miner, ed. (Princeton: Princeton University Press, 1985), pp. 151–180.

Saigyō was no doubt anxious to visit it for that reason, as well as to view its scenery. Another extended trip was to the island of Shikoku, where he paid his respects at the tomb of Emperor Sutoku, who had died there in exile, and at the birthplace of Kūkai, the founder of the Shingon sect in Japan.

In 1180, when fighting broke out between the Taira and Minamoto clans, Saigyō retired to the relative quiet of the Ise region, which he had visited on previous occasions and where he had friends. There he conducted poetry contests with the priests of the famous Shinto shrines at Ise and instructed them in the art of poetry.

In 1186, after peace had been restored, he set off on his second trip to the far north. One purpose of the trip was to raise funds for the rebuilding of the great Tōdai-ji temple in Nara, which had been burned to the ground by the Taira forces in 1180. On his way he stopped in Kamakura, the seat of the newly-established military government of the Minamotos. An often-repeated anecdote in the *Azuma kagami*, a history of the period, states that he was summoned to an interview by Minamoto Yoritomo, the founder of the shogunate. Yoritomo questioned him on matters pertaining to the martial arts, and at the conclusion presented him with a silver image of a cat. When Saigyō emerged from the interview, he handed the silver cat to a child who was playing nearby before proceeding on his way.[2]

After returning to the capital area, Saigyō lived for a time in Saga west of the city, and later moved to a mountain temple called Hirokawa-dera, in Kawachi, south of present-day Osaka. He died there in 1190 at the age of seventy-three by Japanese reckoning. His grave in the temple grounds continues to the present day to be the site of various activities commemorating his life and literary achievement.

With the exception of a few works in *renga* or linked verse form, none of which are translated here, all of Saigyō's poems

---

2. The anecdote is of course meant to impress us with Saigyō's contempt for worldly goods, though for someone who was on a fund-raising tour, it seems a rather foolish act. Anecdotes of this type, which attempt to supplement and lend color to the meager biographical information contained in Saigyō's own writings, apparently began springing up quite early, perhaps even while Saigyō was alive, and in the century following his death swelled to considerable proportions. There is no way at this late date to tell whether such anecdotes have any basis in truth; I have repeated a few of them here only because they are too famous to ignore.

are in the 31-syllable *tanka* or *waka* form, the form most favored in Japanese court poetry. The *Sankashū* or "Mountain Home Collection," which contains the bulk of Saigyō's extant poetry, is arranged by subject rather than chronological order, and relatively few of Saigyō's poems give any indication of their date of composition. It is therefore next to impossible to discuss his works in terms of stylistic development. All we can say with assurance is that, while turning out a large number of poems on conventional themes and in a more or less conventional style, he also labored to create a wholly new style that in time would come to be viewed as characteristic of the late twelfth century as a whole. In doing so, he worked in cooperation with his lifelong friends, the courtier Fujiwara Shunzei (1114–1204), a leading poet of the period and a pioneer in stylistic development, and the latter's son Fujiwara Teika (1162–1241), an equally outstanding poet.

Prior to this, Japanese poetry had twice achieved noteworthy peaks of artistic excellence. The first of these is embodied in the eighth-century anthology known as the *Man'yōshū* or "Collection of Ten Thousand Leaves." The second occurred a century and a half later and is reflected in another famous anthology, the *Kokinshū* or "Collection of Ancient and Modern Times." The *Man'yōshū*, however, because of its archaic diction and the complex and difficult writing system in which it is recorded, exercised little direct influence upon the poetry of the centuries immediately following its appearance. Rather it was the poetry of the *Kokinshū* that became the model for poetic composition in the centuries immediately previous to Saigyō's time.

The poetry of the *Kokinshū* is distinguished for its decorum in subject matter and diction and its air of wit and subjectivity. Chinese loan words, as well as diction that was thought to be unduly colloquial or inelegant, were rigorously shunned, and efforts were made to sustain a tone of purity and elevation in both language and content. Emphasis was upon the poet's response to a particular scene or situation rather than upon the scene itself, with the poet frequently musing upon the process by which he perceives his surroundings. Because of this subjective approach, the poems tend to contain a relatively large number of verbs relating to the poet's feelings and reactions, often in highly inflected forms, and a rather small number of nouns. A smooth, flowing syntax is favored, with frequent use of word plays and other rhetorical devices.

Although there were sporadic attempts at innovation, this *Kokinshū* style remained in vogue down to the time of Shunzei and Saigyō, though in the two centuries following its creation it had lost much of its original vigor and become increasingly shallow and mannered. The time was clearly ripe for some sort of stylistic revolution, and this was what Shunzei and his associates set about to effect.

The new style that they evolved was in many respects the antithesis of the *Kokinshū* manner. In it, the subjective element so prominent in the earlier style was reduced and greater space allotted to description, which resulted in fewer and simpler verb forms and a larger proportion of nouns. The flowing effect prized by previous poets was rejected, the syntax often being deliberately broken in the middle or impeded by fragmentation. Though the diction remained basically conservative, there were efforts, notably by Saigyō, to introduce colloquialisms and to broaden the range of subject matter. Most important, probably as a result of the ominous social and political unrest of the period and the influence of the Buddhist concept of Mappō, the new style was marked by a bleak and somber air quite uncharacteristic of earlier periods, a tendency to favor imagery suggestive of drabness, loneliness, and melancholy, qualities summed up in the Japanese term *sabi*.

To illustrate some of these characteristics as they are reflected in Saigyō's style, or variety of styles, let me cite a few examples. The first is a poem on spring, included in both the *Sankashū* (120) and the *Shinkokinshū* (126), which shows Saigyō writing in the old flowing, highly subjective style typical of the *Kokinshū*:

Nagamu tote	Gazing at them,
hana ni mo itaku	I've grown so very close
narenureba	to these blossoms,
chiru wakare koso	to part with them when they fall
kanashikarikere	seems bitter indeed!

The poem, it will be noted, contains only one image, *hana* or "blossoms," which here designates cherry blossoms; the remainder of the poem is wholly given up to the subjective reflections of the poet. Note also that the third and fifth lines or units of the poem are occupied entirely by inflected verb forms descriptive of the poet's feelings. The poem in fact lacks only a play on words or other rhetorical flourish to be a typical specimen of the old *Kokinshū* style, though a *Kokinshū* poet would probably not have expressed so intense and personal an identification with nature.

The next sample, *Sankashū* 1152, is from the section of the work labeled *zatsu* or "Miscellaneous" and, as the heading indicates, was composed on a *dai* or set theme. Despite this fact, it is clearly a deeply felt work and undoubtedly reflects Saigyō's own experiences and his sincere appreciation of human companionship.

With others, writing on the theme "In Tree Shade, Enjoying the Cool"

Kyō mo mata	Today again
matsu no kaze fuku	I'll go to the hill
oka e yukan	where pine winds blow—
kinō suzumishi	perhaps to meet my friend
tomo ni au ya to	who was cooling himself there yesterday

Here the number of images is much greater—hill, pine winds, friend—and the subjective element less prominent than in the first example. The poem, as often with Saigyō, opens with an exclamation by the poet, direct and conversational in tone, followed, after a pause at the end of the third line, by an explanation of the reason for the initial statement. As a part of his religious training, Saigyō deliberately forced himself to endure isolation and loneliness; yet again and again in his poetry we see this type of longing for companionship breaking through. And where the possibility of human company is lacking, he often seeks fellowship in the creatures of the natural world. Such unabashed confessions of loneliness and the yearning for companionship in fact constitute one of the qualities that readers have found most appealing in Saigyō's poetry, lending it an impulsive warmth and saving it from the studied detachment that marks so much Buddhist poetry in Chinese and Japanese.

The third poem to be cited is one of Saigyō's most famous and often discussed works. It is preserved in both the *Sankashū* (470) and the *Shinkokinshū* (362) and depicts an autumn scene.

Kokoro naki	Even a person free of passion
mi nimo aware wa	would be moved
shirarekeri	to sadness:

shigi tatsu sawa no   autumn evening
aki no yūgure   in a marsh where snipes fly up

This poem, like the previous one, falls into two distinct parts, with a sharp break in syntax at the end of the third line. The first part offers a general observation on the theme of melancholy; the second utilizes four nouns to present a richly imagistic depiction of the autumn scene. The poem ends with a noun, a frequent occurrence in poetry in the new style created by Saigyō and other writers of this time.

The opening phrase, *kokoro naki mi,* means literally "a person without heart/mind." Some commentators believe it denotes a person lacking in sensibility, interpreting it as Saigyō's modest way of alluding to himself, i.e., "even a dull clod like me." The more common interpretation, however, takes it to mean a person who has ceased to be unduly swayed by emotion, one who has reached the state of calm detachment and acceptance that is the goal of Buddhist practice. Saigyō seems to be suggesting that even someone who has attained such a level of detachment could not fail to be moved by the scene before him. He then evokes the scene itself: the stillness of an autumn evening as it is broken by the sudden fluttering up of a snipe or snipes (we have no way to determine whether the poet intended the image to be singular or plural). Something in the fading light, the desolate marsh, the jarring flight of the bird or birds, stirs him so profoundly that he cannot conceive of anyone, even the most disciplined practitioner of Buddhist calm, remaining unmoved in such circumstances.

Here Saigyō, as was often the case with his contemporary poets Shunzei and Teika, has deliberately turned his back on the showier and more patently attractive sights of nature so frequently celebrated in earlier poetry, to focus on a scene that is essentially drab and colorless in nature. Perhaps he and his fellow poets felt that the very drabness of such scenes, their dim half-light and autumnal sadness, more aptly reflected the age of social decline in which they lived than could any brighter and cheerier landscape.

Though we may not be certain exactly what symbolic overtones were conveyed to Saigyō's contemporaries by the poems so far quoted, we may be sure that the natural images employed in them are intended to function on the metaphorical as well as the literal level. In some of his works, however, Saigyō appears to have abandoned the conventions of Japanese court poetry altogether and experimented in producing works of pure description. He was greatly aided in such experiments by the fact that his travels took him to areas of the country not ordinarily visited, by the court poets, where he could view scenes scarcely even touched on in earlier poetry. Here, for example, is a poem—from the "Miscellaneous" section of the *Sankashū* (1380)—that was evidently written on a trip to the Inland Sea and Ise region, perhaps around 1167:

Amabito no	Fishermen home from
isoshiku kaeru	their day's work:
hijiki mono wa	on a bed of seaweed,
konishi hamaguri	little top shells, clams,
gōna shitadami	hermit crabs, periwinkles

Perhaps, as is often the case with Saigyō's poems on fisherfolk, the poem is intended as a reproach to these men and women whose daily livelihood involves the taking of life, though such a sentiment is nowhere expressed in the poem. Rather the poet seems to be taking a kind of childlike delight in peering into the fishermen's baskets and learning the names of the shellfish and crustaceans they contain, a delight perhaps intended to illustrate the assertion that all creatures of the universe, no matter how lowly, are embodiments of the Buddhist Law. Aristocrat readers and writers of poetry residing in the capital at this time would have been fully equipped to appreciate the significance of images such as cuckoos and bush warblers, kerria roses or pampas grass, for they had mastered the allusions and poetic lore associated with these images. But what could they possibly have made of Saigyō's hermit crabs and periwinkles? Yet the fact that a poet of Saigyō's stature ventured to write on such lowly and unconventional objects was of great significance to the later development of Japanese poetry. In doing so, he helped to broaden the scope and conventions of court poetry and to open up new paths for the *renga* and *haikai* poets of the centuries that were to follow.

Because of his extensive travels, Saigyō had an opportunity to visit a number of the so-called *uta-makura*, places famed for some particularly noteworthy natural feature or sight, and to write poems on them. Such spots were regarded as especially appropriate for poetic treatment, and later poets visiting them often alluded in their works to earlier compositions on the subject. Thus, in his journeys to northern Japan, Saigyō took care to visit and write on places earlier treated by the monk-poet Nōin, whom Saigyō greatly admired. Still later, it became the practice to inscribe on stone the poems composed at these sites and set them up as testimonials of literary activity, so that today such *uta-makura* fairly bristle with poetic monuments.

In addition to poems on conventional sights and themes, Saigyō, because of his commitment to religious life, wrote a number of poems on specifically Buddhist topics, paraphrasing passages of scripture or meditating on the principles of the Law, so that in this respect his works differ somewhat from those of purely secular writers of the period. He is also noted for the frequency with which he runs over the prescribed number of syllables in a line, particularly in the first line, or for ignoring the prohibition against employing the same word twice in a single poem—see, for example, the poem on page 219, which uses the verb *sutsuru*, "to cast off," a total of four times. His poetry in fact at times displays a freedom and indifference to convention that was probably quite beyond the imagination of more custom-bound poets of the time. In addition, like many of the great Japanese poets, he was not afraid of saying something very simple. [3]

In Saigyō's younger years, his poetry undoubtedly circulated in manuscript and was known to some extent in both court and religious circles. The first official recognition of his work came with the compilation of an imperially sponsored anthology called the *Shikashū* or "Collection of Verbal Flowers." Compiled around the years from 1151 to 1154, it included one poem by Saigyō, that already cited in the paragraph above. The poem was listed as *yomibito shirazu* or "author

---

3. In stressing the simplicity, directness, and originality of Saigyō's poetry, and in presenting translations of his poems without in most cases describing the conventions upon which they draw, I am perhaps in danger of making Saigyō's poetry appear more unconventional than it actually is. Where Saigyō is directly alluding in his work to an earlier poem or text, I have explained the allusion. But it is impossible to explain for each poem the vast body of older usages that underlies its images and sentiments. Suffice it to say that in the selection that follows, what in English translation may appear to be a straight-forward description of a natural scene is often in fact an elaborately "intertextual" reworking of conventional phrases and images, a fact that would have been quite apparent to readers of his time who were familiar with the texts and conventions that he drew upon, On this question of the allusive nature of the poetry of this period, see Haruo Shirane, "Lyricism and Intertextuality: An Approach to Shunzei's Poetics," *Harvard Journal of Asiatic Studies* (June 1990), (50)1:77–85. Professor Shirane's discussion centers on the poetry of Shunzei, but much of what he says could apply equally to that of Saigyō.

unknown," probably because of Saigyō's relatively low social position, though the people who were of importance in poetry circles were most likely quite aware of the author's identity. Interesting as it is, it is hardly representative of his work as a whole.

A far greater degree of artistic recognition came to him some thirty years later with the compilation of another imperial anthology, the *Senzaishū* or "Collection of a Thousand Years," which was begun in 1183 and completed in 1188. It was compiled by Saigyō's lifelong friend Fujiwara Shunzei and included eighteen poems by Saigyō.

Uta-awase or poetry contests, in which two teams competed in composing poems on stated topics, were a frequent and highly serious feature of the literary life of the period. In addition, poets engaged in *jika-awase* or personal poetry competitions, arranging their own poems in pairs, each pair dealing with a single topic, as though they were the work of competing writers, and often inviting a friend or associate to judge which of the two poems in each pair should be regarded as the winner. Saigyō put together two such sequences of poems, both named for rivers in the Ise region where he was living at the time, the *Mimosusogawa uta-awase* or "Poetry Contest at the Mimosuso River," compiled in 1187, and the *Miyagawa uta-awase* or "Poetry Contest at the Miya River," compiled in 1189. He sent the former to Fujiwara Shunzei and the latter to Shunzei's son Teika for judgment. Their judgments and critical comments have been preserved and indicate the high esteem in which these men held Saigyō's work.

When Saigyō died in 1190, he must have known that he had carved out for himself a position of lasting importance in the history of Japanese poetry. Whether he could possibly have foreseen the overwhelming prominence that would be conferred upon his poetry with the compilation of the *Shinkokinshū* some sixteen years later, we can only speculate.

It is not known just when or by whom the *Sankashū* or "Mountain Home Collection" was compiled, though it appears to date from Saigyō's lifetime and may well have been compiled by Saigyō himself. It contains about 1550 poems—the number varies somewhat with different versions of the text. Not all are by Saigyō, as the collection includes exchanges of poems carried out between Saigyō and his friends. The poems are arranged by topic, beginning with sections devoted to the four seasons, followed by a group of love poems, and ending with a section entitled "Miscellaneous" that has apparently been added to at a later date and represents a catchall for poems that do not fit easily into other categories.

Western readers may wonder what a section on love poems is doing in the collected works of a man who was a Buddhist monk for almost all of his adult life. But the theme of romantic love, particularly as it progresses stage by stage in the psychological attitude of the participants, was one of the most frequent topics in Japanese court poetry, and anyone with pretensions to being a serious poet would be expected to produce works dealing with it. Some of Saigyō's love poems may date from the years before he entered religious life, but it is clear that he continued to compose on the subject throughout the remainder of his years. Many of the love poems are written from the woman's point of view, a common convention in love poetry even when composed by men. There is a possibility that some of the love poems, like some of the poems in other categories that are quite unrelated to religion, are in fact intended to convey a deep religious meaning.

The *Sankashū* appears to contain the bulk of Saigyō's poems written up to about 1180, but it does not by any means include all his extant poems. The ninety-four poems by Saigyō preserved in the *Shinkokinshū* include many that are not found in the *Sankashū*. In making my selection, I have therefore drawn from both the *Sankashū* and *Shinkokinshū*, as well as from several other imperial anthologies. Since the poems in the *Shinkokinshū* are arranged in categories similar to those used in the *Sankashū*, I have placed poems from the former with those from the latter that belong to the same category, except that the *Shinkokinshū* includes sections on travel poems and Shinto poems that have no counterpart in the *Sankashū*. For expedience sake, I have placed poems from these last two sections in the "Miscellaneous" section.

Poets of Saigyō's time often composed poems on *dai* or topics expressed in a two-character or four-character phrase in Chinese such as "New Greens" or "Winter Deepens in a Mountain Home." In order to make such topics in Chinese readily identifiable, I have capitalized the principal words. Where the heading of the original poem is in Japanese, I have capitalized only the first word. Headings in the original that contribute nothing to the reader's understanding of the poem, such as *Dai shirazu* or "Topic unknown," I have simply omitted in translation.

In 1929 a short text known as the *Kikigaki shū*, containing 263 poems by Saigyō, none of which are found in the *Sankashū*, was discovered. It includes several groups of poems such as that written "In a light vein" that date from Saigyō's late years and are of unusual interest because of their colloquial diction and the insight they give into Saigyō's personality. I have ended my selection with examples from this text.

My translations from the *Sankashū* are based on the texts found in Kazamaki Keijirō and Kojima Yoshio, *Sankashū, Kinkai wakashū*, Nihon koten bungaku taikei 29 (Tokyo: Iwanami shoten, 1961), and Gotō Shigeo, *Sankashū*, Shinchō Nihon koten shūsei (Tokyo: Shinchōsha, 1982). The text of the *Kikigaki shū* is found on pp. 274–289 of the former work. My translations from the *Shinkokinshū* are based on the text in Minemura Fumito, *Shinkokin wakashū*, Nihon koten bungaku zenshū (Tokyo: Shōgakkan, 1974). The numbers in parentheses that follow the romanized texts in my selection refer to the poems as they are numbered in these works. The abbreviation SKS refers to the *Sankashū* and SKKS to the *Shinkokinshū*. The romanized versions of the poems are meant simply as guides to readers or students of Japanese who wish to visualize the originals; they are not intended to represent the poems as they were pronounced in Saigyō's time.

Readers of English who want to read further on Saigyō should consult the sections on Saigyō and his contemporaries in Robert H. Brower and Earl Miner, *Japanese Court Poetry* (Stanford: Stanford University Press, 1961) and the translation of 173 Saigyō's poems by William R. LaFleur, *Mirror for the Moon* (New York: New Directions, 1978), which contains an excellent introduction. There is a complete English translation of the *Sankashū* by H. H. Honda, *The Sanka Shu* (Tokyo: Hokuseido Press, 1971), but the introduction and notes are minimal and the translations indescribably drab.

Some of my translations appeared earlier in the anthology of Japanese poetry entitled *From the Country of Eight Islands*, Hiroaki Sato and Burton Watson (New York: Doubleday, 1981; Columbia University Press, 1986), and are included here in somewhat revised form.

In addition to the works cited above, I have drawn on the following works for material in the introduction and notes:

Ishida Yoshisada, *Inja no bungaku*, Hanawa shinshō 17 (Tokyo: Hanawa shobō, 1969).

Kawada Jun, *Saigyō shū*, in *Sanetomo shū, Saigyō shū, Ryōkan shū*, Koten Nihon bungaku zenshū 21 (Tokyo: Chikuma shobō, 1960).

Kubota Jun, *Sankashū* (Tokyo: Iwanami shoten, 1983).

Mezaki Tokue, *Saigyō no shisōshi-teki kenkyū* (Tokyo: Yoshikawa kōbunkan, 1978).

Watanabe Tamotsu, *Saigyō Sankashū zenchūkai* (Tokyo: Kazama shobō, 1971).

Yamada Shōzen, *Saigyō no waka to Bukkyō* (Tokyo: Meiji shoin, 1987).

Yamaki Kōichi, *Saigyō no sekai*, Hanawa shinsho 53 (Tokyo: Hanawa shobō, 1979).

Yamaki Kōichi, *Saigyō waka no keisei to juyō* (Tokyo: Meiji shoin, 1987).

S
P
R
I
N
G

Spring

❀

Ice wedged fast

in the crevice of the rock

this morning begins to melt—

under the moss the water

will be feeling out a channel

∿

Iwama tojishi   kōri mo kesa wa   tokesomete
koke no shita mizu   michi motomuran
SKKS 1 (7)

Spring

The deep snow that

fell and piled up on the high peaks

has melted:

white waves dot the flow

of Clear Torrent River*

.~.

Furi tsumishi   takane no miyuki   tokenikeri
kiyotakigawa no   mizu no shiranami
SKKS 1 (27)

* Kiyotakigawa or Clear Torrent River flows through
the hills west of Kyoto.

Spring

❀

You can tell

from the outline of the hills,

the way it's hazed over—

from this morning on

we'll have springtime dawns*

·〜·

Yama no ha no   kasumu keshiki ni   shiruki kana
kesa yori ya sa wa   haru no akebono
SKS 1 (2)

* Said by Sei Shōnagon in the opening of her *Pillow Book* to be the most beautiful dawns of the year.

Spring

❀

Seashore Haze

There on the shore

where they're boiling seaweed salt,

the rising smoke lingers,

rises up and mingles

with the spring haze*

٠ᴗ٠

Moshio yaku   ura no atari wa   tachinokade
kemuri tachisou   haru kasumi kana
SKS 1 (12)

* Seawater was poured over racks of seaweed and the water dripping down was then boiled to extract the salt, a common method of salt production.

Spring

❀

New Greens

While the old year lasted,

Kasuga Field

was buried in snow.

Now it's spring

and new shoots are poking up *

⌣

Kasugano wa   toshi no uchi ni wa   yuki tsumite
haru wa wakana no   ouru narikeri
SKS 1 (19)

* On the seventh day of the New Year, people gath-
ered the shoots of herbs and prepared a seven-herb rice
gruel that was believed to ward off illness throughout
the year. Kasuga Field in Nara was a well-known spot
for gathering such herbs. The poem plays on *tsumu*, "to
pile up" as of now, and *tsumu*, "to pluck" as of shoots.

23

Spring

On young herbs, thinking of the past

Sad the haze in the meadow

where I pick young herbs

when I think

how it shrouds me

from the faraway past

Wakana tsumu   nobe no kasumi zo   aware naru

mukashi o tōku   hedatsu to omoeba

SKS 1 (21)

Spring

❀

The Bush Warbler Idling

Seeping through the haze,

the voice

of the bush warbler—

few people passing,

mountain village in spring

～

Uguisu no   koe zo kasumi ni   morete kuru
hitome tomoshiki   haru no yamazato*
SKS 1 (25)

* *Yamazato* or "mountain village" usually designates a
small community or settlement in the mountains. But
Saigyō often seems to be using it to refer to a single
mountain dwelling where he lives alone in retirement.
In his poetry the word has strong connotations of isolation and loneliness.

Spring

❀

Pheasant

It sounds as though

he's hunting

new shoots that've sprouted—

pheasant crying in the field

in springtime dawn

·〜·

Moe izuru   wakana asaru to   kikoyu nari
kigisu naku no no   haru no akebono
SKS 1 (31)

Spring

❀

The Plum Tree at My Mountain Hut

Take note:

the plum by my rustic hedge

halted in his tracks

a total stranger

who happened by

∽·

Kokoro sen   shizu ga kakine no   mume wa aya na

yoshi naku suguru   hito todomekeri

SKS 1 (36)

Spring

This spring I'll stay

close to my rustic hedge,

make friends

with people who come

in search of the plum's fragrance

·∿·

Kono haru wa   shizu ga kakine ni   furebaite
mume ga ka tomen   hito shitashiman
SKS 1 (37)

Spring

❀

*When I was living in Saga, the wind would
scatter plum blossoms from the monk's lodging
across the road.*

How the owner

must hate it

when the wind blows,

though over here, pure joy

in the fragrance of the plum

·～·

Nushi ika ni   kaze wataru tote   itouran

yoso ni ureshiki   mume no nioi o

SKS 1 (38)

Spring

❀

Spring Showers in a Mountain Dwelling—written at Ōhara

Curtained by spring showers

pouring down from the eaves,

a place where someone lives,

idle, idle,

unknown to others

⌣

Harusame no   noki tarekomuru   tsurezure ni
hito ni shirarenu   hito no sumika ka
SKS 1 (45)

❀

Rice Seedling Beds

Mist seems to

draw the water, leading it

into seedling beds,

as it hovers above

the irrigation troughs

～

Nawashiro no   mizu o kasumi wa   tanabikite
uchihi no ue ni   kakuru narikeri
SKS 1 (50)

Mountain Home Willow

Poor people of the hills,

a piece of the long slope

taken over for their shack,

and as though for a boundary,

that jewel of a young willow!

Yamagatsu no   kataoka kakete   shimuru io no
sakai ni miyuru   tama no oyanagi
SKS 1 (52)

❀

Willow in the Rain

Tangled even further

in the wind

that dries them—

threads of green willow

wet with rain

·◝·

Naka naka ni   kaze no hosu ni zo   midarekeru
ame ni nuretaru   aoyagi no ito
SKS 1 (53)

Spring

❀

On Mount Yoshino

snowflakes scattering down

from cherry limbs—

one of those years

when blossoms will come late*

·~·

Yoshinoyama   sakura ga eda ni   yuki chirite
hana osoge naru   toshi ni mo aru kana
SKKS 1 (79)

* Mount Yoshino, in Nara Prefecture south of the city
of Nara, is the site of several famous temples and shrines
and is noted for the thousands of cherry trees that
bloom in spring on the mountain. Saigyō frequently
visited it and for a time lived in a hut there.

3 4

I'll forget the trail

I marked out on Mount Yoshino

last year,

go searching for blossoms

in directions I've never been before

~

Yoshinoyama   kozo no shiori no   michi kaete
mada minu kata no   hana o tazunen
SKKS 1 (86)

Spring

Since the day I saw

Mount Yoshino's

blossoming treetops,

my body's one place,

my heart in another

·~·

Yoshinoyama   kozue no hana o   mishi hi yori

kokoro wa mi ni mo   sowazu nariniki

SKS 1 (66)

Spring

I'd have it first one way, then the reverse—

in blossom-viewing spring,

never mind nighttime,

in moon-viewing autumn,

do away with days!

·〜·

Hikikaete hana miru haru wa yoru wa naku
tsuki miru aki wa hiru nakaranan
SKS 1 (71)

Spring

If only I could

divide myself,

not miss a single tree,

see the blossoms at their best

on all ten thousand mountains!*

·〜·

Mi o wakete   minu kozue naku   tsukusaba ya

yorozu no yama no   hana no sakari o

SKS 1 (74)

* The conceit of dividing the body into countless selves
derives from Buddhist scriptures, in which the Buddhas
are frequently depicted doing this. Saigyō perhaps borrowed it from the four-line poem by the Chinese poet
Liu Tsung-yüan (773-819) entitled "A Poem to Send to
Friends in the Capital," the closing lines of which read:

　If I could change into a million selves
　I'd send one to climb each peak and gaze far off
　toward home.

See my *Columbia Book of Chinese Poetry* (New York: Columbia University Press, 1984), p. 282.

Spring

Why should my heart

still harbor

this passion for cherry flowers,

I who thought

I had put all that behind me?

Hana ni somu   kokoro no ika de   nokoriken
sute hateteki to   omou waga mi ni
SKS 1 (76)

Spring

❀

Let me die in spring

under the blossoming trees,

let it be around

that full moon

of Kisaragi month*

·～·

Negawaku wa   hana no shita nite   haru shinan
sono kisaragi no   mochizuki no koro
SKS 1 (77)

* Kisaragi is the Japanese name for the second month
of the lunar year. Shakyamuni Buddha is said to have
died on the fifteenth day of the second month. Saigyō
fulfilled the wish expressed in his poem in a striking
manner by dying on the sixteenth day of the second
month of 1190, a feat that greatly impressed the people
of his time, who were familiar with this poem.

Spring

❀

To the dead

make offerings

of cherry flowers—

so I would say if someone

were to mourn me when I'm gone

·〜·

Hotoke* ni wa   sakura no hana o   tatematsure
waga nochi no yo o   hito toburawaba
SKS 1 (78)

* *Hotoke* means literally "a Buddha," but it is used in
common parlance to refer to a deceased person, since
according to Amidist belief all who die in the faith will
in time attain Buddhahood.

Spring

❀

Viewing cherries in the spring dawn and hearing a bush warbler's call

The color of the blossoms

must be dyed in that sound—

a warbler's call

lovelier than ever

in spring dawn

〜

Hana no iro ya   koe ni somuran   uguisu no
naku ne kotonaru   haru no akebono
SKS 1 (91)

Spring

Take a good look:

even the blossoms

of the old cherry seem sad—

how many more times

will they see the spring?

Wakite min   oiki wa hana mo   aware nari
ima ikutabi ka   haru ni aubeki
SKS 1 (94)

❀

Mountain Path, Fallen Blossoms

First snowfall

of cherry petals

starting to scatter—

how hateful, tramping through it

over the pass from Shiga!*

〜

Chiri somuru   hana no hatsuyuki   furinureba
fumiwake ma uki   shiga no yamagoe
SKS 1 (105)

* Shiga is the Lake Biwa area beyond the mountains
east of Kyoto.

Spring

Gazing at them,

I've grown so very close

to these blossoms,

to part with them when they fall

seems bitter indeed!

Nagamu tote   hana ni mo itaku   narenureba
chiru wakare koso   kanashikarikere
SKS 1 (120); SKKS 2 (126)

Spring

Recalling blossoms after they've scattered

Once I see

the new green leaves,

my heart may take to them too—

if I think of them as mementos

of blossoms that scattered

·~·

Aoba sae   mireba kokoro no   tomaru kana
chirinishi hana no   nagori to omoeba
SKS 1 (158)

Violets

Never visited,

the whole garden rank with

low-growing cogon grass—

who pushed a way through,

coming to pick violets?

∽

Ato taete   asaji shigereru   niwa no omo ni
tare wakeirite   sumire tsumiten
SKS 1 (159)

Azaleas on a Mountain Trail

Moving from rock to rock,

I clutch at azaleas,

but not to pick them—

on these steep slopes

I count on them for a handhold

⁓

Iwa tsutai   orade tsutsuji o   te ni zo toru
sagashiki yama no   toridokoro ni wa
SKS 1 (163)

Kerria Rose

How hateful of someone

to have planted them

so close to the riverbank! —

sprays of kerria rose

broken by the waves*

Kishi chikami   ueken hito zo   urameshiki
nami ni oraruru   yamabuki no hana
SKS 1 (165)

* The *yamabuki* or kerria rose is a large bush with showy
yellow flowers that blooms in late spring. Those growing along the Tama River at Ide south of Kyoto are
frequently mentioned in early Japanese poetry. Watanabe Tamotsu in his commentary on the poem asserts
that Saigyō is concerned not that the actual sprays of
the plant will be broken in the water, but that their
reflection will be distorted by the ripples. The original,
which says "blossoms of the kerria rose," may be taken
either way.

❀

Frogs

When we flood

the mountain paddies

grown over with sedge grass,

what joyful faces

on the croaking frogs!

꒭

Masuge ouru   yamada ni mizu o   makasureba
ureshigao ni mo   naku kawazu kana
SKS 1 (167)

Frogs

Muddy inlet

so scummy even moonlight

won't linger there—

it's home to us!

say the croaking frogs

Misabi ite   tsuki mo yadoranu   nigorie ni
ware suman tote   kawazu naku nari*
SKS 1 (168)

* There is a play on *sumu,* "to live," and *sumu,* "to be clear."

S
U
M
M
E
R

Cuckoo—

I've yet to hear him

but I'll wait for him here

in this stand of dense cedars

on Yamada moor*

⌣

Kikazu tomo   koko o se ni sen   hototogisu
yamada no hara no   sugi no muradachi
SKKS 3 (217)

* Yamada moor is near the Ise Shrine, in the area
where Saigyō lived in his late years.

Summer

Cuckoo has emerged

from his faraway

mountain peak—

along the rim of the foothills

his note comes drifting down

.∾.

Hototogisu   fukaki mine yori   idenikeri
toyama no suso ni   koe no ochikuru
SKKS 3 (218)

Evening Cuckoo

The twilight cuckoo

now quite at home in our village—

I pretend not to hear,

hoping to make him

speak his name again

Sato naruru   tasogaredoki no   hototogisu
kikazugao nite   mata nanorasen
SKS 1 (181)

Rock-damned marsh—

in fifth-month rains

so full of water

you can't pick your way

over the stones any longer

Samidare wa   iwa seku numa no   mizu fukami
wakeshi ishima no   kayoido mo nashi
SKS 1 (209)

S u m m e r

Staring blankly

at the drops

from rafter ends,

barely getting through the days—

fifth-month rainy season

Tsukuzuku to   noki no shizuku o   nagametsutsu
hi o nomi kurasu   samidare no koro
SKS 1 (211)

In fifth-month rains

no trace of a path

where I can make my way,

meadows of bamboo grass

awash in muddy water

⋅➤⋅

Samidare wa   yukubeki michi no   ate mo nashi
ozasa ga hara mo   uki ni nagarete
SKS 1 (226)

In willow shade

where clear water flows

by the wayside—

"Just a while!" I said

as I stopped to rest

⋅∿⋅

Michi no be ni   shimizu nagaruru   yanagi kage
shibashi tote kōso   tachidomaritsure
SKKS 3 (262)

Across the face of the field

wilted grasses

darken:

the chill clouding-over

of a sudden storm sky

Yoraretsuru   nomose no kusa no   kageroite

suzushiku kumoru   yūdachi no sora

SKKS 3 (263)

Traveler Passing Where Grasses Are Deep

Traveler pushing his way

through a summer meadow,

grasses so thick

his sedge hat seems

to float over their tips

᠅

Tabibito no   wakuru natsuno no   kusa shigemi
hazue ni suge no   ogasa hazurete
SKS 1 (237)

S u m m e r

Summer nights I doubt

they can even see the moon—

poor people in their lean-to,

burning smudge fires

to keep off the mosquitoes

Natsu no yo no   tsuki miru koto ya   nakaruran

kayaribi tatsuru   shizu no fuseya wa

SKS 1 (241)

A
U
T
U
M
N

Even in a person

most times indifferent

to things around him

they waken feelings—

the first winds of autumn

·◞·

Oshinabete   mono o omowanu   hito ni sae
kokoro o tsukuru   aki no hatsukaze
SKKS 4 (299)

Autumn

Ah, how many drops of dew

will spill

from leaves of grass—

fall winds are rising

on Miyagino plain *

·ゝ·

Aware ika ni kusaba no tsuyu no   koboruran

akikaze tachinu   miyagino no hara

SKKS 4 (300)

---

* The plain of Miyagino in the Sendai area of northern Japan is famous for its bush clover and other autumn-blooming plants.

Pampas Grass Thick on the Path

With blooms of pampas grass

for markers

I push my way along,

no trace of the trail

I vaguely remembered

᠁

Hana susuki   kokoro ate ni zo   wakete yuku
hono mishi michi no   ato shi nakereba
SKS 1 (274)

Reeds

Sounding even

more mournful

than I'd expected,

an autumn evening wind

tossing in the reed leaves

∿

Omou ni mo   sugite aware ni   kikoyuru wa
ogi no ha midaru   aki no yūkaze
SKS 1 (285)

How lonely, the light of the moon

filtering into my hut,

the only sound, the clackers

that shoo away birds

in the mountain paddies

Io ni moru   tsuki no kage koso   sabishikere
yamada wa hita no   oto bakari shite
SKS 1 (303)

I used to gaze at the moon,

my mind wandering endlessly —

and now again

I've come on one of

those old time autumns

Tsuki o mite   kokoro ukareshi   inishie no

aki ni mo sara ni   meguri ainuru

SKS 1 (349), SKKS 16 (1530)

A u t u m n

When I was paying my respects at Kasuga,
the moon was even brighter than usual and I
*was moved to write this.**

Gazing at this moon

over Mikasa tonight,

I know how he must have felt,

that man who

"looked far off"

.

Furi sakeshi   hito no kokoro zo   shirarenuru
koyoi mikasa no   tsuki o nagamete
SKS 1 (407)

* Kasuga is a famous Shinto shrine at the foot of Mount
Mikasa in Nara. Saigyō is recalling a poem by Abe no
Nakamarō (701–770), an envoy to the T'ang court in
China during the Nara period. Abe wrote the poem in
China in 752, when he was about to board a ship to
return to Japan. The poem expresses his longing for his
homeland, and is preserved in *Kokinshū* 9 (406).

Ama no hara	I turn to look
furisake mireba	far off at the sky—
kasuga naru	the same moon
mikasa no yama ni	that used to rise
ideshi tsuki ka mo	over Mount Mikasa in Kasuga!

Abe's poem is especially poignant in view of the fact
that, after he had embarked for Japan, his ship was
blown far off course and wrecked on the China coast.
He made his way back to the T'ang capital but died
there without ever returning to Japan.

Hearing Wild Geese at Dawn

As banked clouds

are swept apart

by the wind at dawn,

the cry of the first wild geese

winging over the mountain

·✄·

Yokogumo no   kaze ni wakaruru   shinonome ni

yama tobikoyuru   hatsukari no koe

SKS 1 (420), SKKS 5 (501)

The Moon Seen on a Journey

Moon-viewings in the capital

when I thought

such sad thoughts —

now I know they were no more

than idle pastimes

Miyako nite   tsuki o aware to   omoishi wa
kazu yori hoka no   susabi narikeri
SKS 1 (418); SKKS 10 (937)

The Call of Wild Geese Far and Near

Wild geese departing,

their wings in white clouds,

call longingly to their friends

in the paddies

outside my gate

·◟·

Shirakumo o   tsubasa ni kakete   yuku kari no

kadoda no omo no   tomo shitau nari

SKS 1 (422); SKKS 5 (502)

Autumn, when even

without it

all things seem mournful,

the sound of the stag's cry

brings tears welling up

⤳

Saranu dani   aki wa mono nomi   kanashiki o
namida moyōsu   saoshika no koe
SKS 1 (432)

Insects in the Rain

In the little weeds

that sprout in my wall

a cricket wails—

he must be peeved at the dew

that soaks the garden

.~.

Kabe ni ouru   kogusa ni waburu   kirigirisu

shigururu niwa no   tsuyu itoubeshi

SKS 1 (461)

Insects on an Evening Road

On the road with not a soul

to keep me company,

as evening falls

katydids lift their voices

and cheer me along

٠ᴖ٠

Uchigusuru   hito naki michi no   yūsare wa
koe nite okuru   kutsuwamushi kana*
SKS 1 (463)

* For the first phrase, I follow the reading in the *Rokkashū* text. The insect is called *kutsuwamushi* or "horse-bit
bug" because its cry suggests the sound of a bit in a
horse's mouth; hence the traveler in the poem feels as
though he has company on the road.

A u t u m n

So deep into autumn

their fellow flowers

are all gone—

if the frost would only hold off,

leave me the incomparable chrysanthemums!

`◝◜`

Aki fukami   narabu hana naki   kiku nareba
tokoro o shimo no   oke to koso omoe
SKS 1 (468)

Autumn

Even a person free of passion

would be moved

to sadness:

autumn evening

in a marsh where snipes fly up

⋅~⋅

Kokoro naki　mi nimo aware wa　shirarekeri
shigi tatsu sawa no　aki no yūgure
SKS 1 (470); SKKS 4 (362)

Crickets—

as the cold of night

deepens into autumn

are you weakening? your voices

grow farther and farther away

·╲·

Kirigirisu   yosamu ni aki no   naru mama ni

yowaru ka koe no   tōzakari yuku

SKKS 5 (472)

A mountain village

at autumn's end—

that's when you learn

what mournfulness means

in the blast of the wintry wind

Yamazato wa aki no sue ni zo omoi shiru
kanashikarikeri kogarashi no kaze
SKS 1 (487)

A u t u m n

All night long regretting the end of autumn

Regret as I may,

even the bell

has a different sound now,

and soon frost will fall

in place of morning dew

·～·

Oshimedomo   kane no oto sae   kawaru kana

shimo ni ya tsuyu o   musubi kauran

SKS 1 (490)

W
I
N
T
E
R

Winter

Clouds have all scattered

from the tall peak

where I wait for moonrise—

what kindness in the first

of these early winter showers!

Tsuki o matsu   takane no kumo wa   harenikeri
kokoro arubeki   hatsushigure kana
SKKS 6 (570)

In Akishino

is it raining

in the foothill villages?

Clouds hang over

Ikoma's peak*

⌒

Akishino ya   toyama no sato ya   shigururan
ikoma no take ni   kumo no kakareru
SKKS 6 (585)

* Akishino is west of the city of Nara. Mount Ikoma
separates Nara from the Osaka area.

Winter

Leaves have fallen

in this village

at the foot of Mount Ogura

and I can see the moon

shining in the tops of the trees*

Ogurayama   fumoto no sato ni   ko no ha chireba
kozue ni haruru   tsuki o miru kana
SKKS 6 (603)

* Mount Ogura is in the hills west of Kyoto.

Was it a dream,

that spring in Naniwa

in the land of Tsu?

Now the wind blows over

the dead leaves of the reeds*

⌁

Tsu no kuni no   naniwa no haru wa   yume nare ya
ashi no kareha ni   kaze wataru nari
SKKS 6 (625)

* Naniwa is the area of the present-day city of Osaka.
Saigyō is alluding to an earlier poem by Priest Nōin
(998–1050) preserved in *Goshūishū* 1 (43):

Kokoro aran	If only I could show them
hito ni miseba ya	to someone of real feeling—
tsu no kuni no	the sights of spring
naniwa watari no	hereabouts in Naniwa
haru no keshiki o	in the land of Tsu!

Falling Leaves at Dawn

Wondering if it's a winter shower,

I wake in my bed

and hear them—

the leaves that

couldn't withstand the storm

Shigure ka to   nezame no toko ni   kikoyuru wa
arashi ni taenu   ko no ha narikeri
SKS 1 (496)

On the theme "Cold Grasses in the Field," written at Sōrin-ji*

Fields we saw

blooming with

so many different flowers,

frost-withered now

to a single hue

⸱◡⸱

Samazama ni   hana sakikeri to   mishi nobe no
onaji iro ni mo   shimogarenikeru
SKS 1 (506)

* A temple in the eastern hills of Kyoto where Saigyō
lived for a time.

W i n t e r

If only there were

someone else

willing to bear this loneliness —

side by side we'd build our huts

for winter in a mountain village

∿

Sabishisa ni   taetaru hito no   mata mo are na
iori naraban   fuyu no yamazato
SKS 1 (513); SKKS 6 (627)

Winter

Neglectful, we've yet

to fix the towrope

to the sled—

and here they're piled up already,

the white snows of Koshi!*

Tayumitsutsu   sori no hayao mo   tsukenaku ni
tsumorinikeru na   koshi no shirayuki
SKS 1 (529)

* Koshi is the Japan Sea coastal area, noted for its
heavy snows.

94

Snow Buries the Bamboo

Heaped with snow,

bamboos in the garden

bend and topple—

flocks of sparrows hunting

for another roost

∙∽∙

Yuki uzumu   sono no kuretake   orefushite
negura motomuru   murasuzume kana
SKS 1 (535)

Boat in a Hailstorm

Little boat with no treadboard

crossing the straits,

take care!

The hail pelts wildly

and the swift wind sweeps in

Seto wataru tana nashi obune kokoro seyo
arare midaruru shimaki yokogiru
SKS 1 (544)

Hail Deep in the Mountains

Woodcutter

sleeping all alone

in his pine bough shelter,

the only sound,

his only visitor, the hail

·∾·

Somabito no   maki no kariya no   adabushi ni
oto suru mono wa   arare narikeri*
SKS 1 (545)

* There is a play on *oto suru*, "to make a sound," and
otozuru, "to visit."

Living alone

in the shade of a remote mountain,

I have you for my companion

now the storm has passed,

moon of the winter night!

Hitori sumu   katayama kage no   tomo nare ya
arashi ni haruru   fuyu no yo no tsuki*
SKS 1 (558)

* The last phrase follows the reading in the *Rokkashū*
text.

Winter Deepens in a Mountain Home

At the first snowfall, yes,

some visitors pushed their way through,

but now all trails

are cut off

to this village deep in the mountains

Tou hito wa   hatsuyuki o koso   wakekoshi ka
michi tojitekeri   miyamabe no sato
SKS 1 (569)

*At year end, sent to a certain person**

Without having to be asked,

I thought the person would come

out of kindness,

but while I was hesitating,

the year came to an end

·〜·

Onozu kara   iwanu o shitau   hito ya aru to
yasurau hodo ni   toshi no kurenuru
SKS 1 (576), SKKS 6 (691)

* According to one interpretation, the "certain person"
was Saigyō's former wife.

Winter

Mount Arachi so steep,

no ravine to descend by,

but the white snow

offers us

a snowshoe trail

⌒

Arachiyama   sakashiku kudaru   tani mo naku
kajiki no michi o   tsukuru shirayuki*
SKS 1 (577)

* This poem is found only in certain versions of the
Rokkashū text; see *Sankashū* (Nihon koten bungaku taikei
29), p. 269. Mount Arachi is in present-day Fukui Prefecture.

Winter

A garden that recalls the past,

but in it I stack

driftwood for fuel—

hardly the kind of year-end

I used to know*

.⌣.

Mukashi omou   niwa no ukigi o   tsumiokite
mishi yo ni mo ninu   toshi no kure kana
SKKS 6 (697)

* Some commentators see in the word "driftwood" an
allusion to the Buddhist parable, found in the *Lotus Sutra*
and elsewhere, that likens the difficulty of attaining
enlightenment to that of a blind turtle encountering a
piece of driftwood to which it can cling. I.e., "stacking
driftwood" here stands for religious endeavor.

L
O
V
E

L o v e

Moon at break of day,

what memories it wakes

of times when I lingered

like the banked clouds

that trail away in the dawn sky*

Ariake wa   omoiide are ya   yokogumo no
tadayowatetsuru   shinonome no sora
SKKS 13 (1193)

* The moon recalls to the speaker times when the
lovers parted at dawn.

L o v e

He never came—

the wind too tells

how the night has worn away,

while mournfully the cries of wild geese

approach and pass on

·~·

Hito wa kode   kaze no keshiki mo   fukenuru ni
aware ni kari no   otozurete yuku
SKKS 13 (1200)

L o v e

No promises—yet I wait,

thinking perhaps you'll come.

If only the night

wouldn't dwindle away

but be over all at once!

Tanomenu ni   kimi ku ya to matsu   yoi no ma no
fukeyukade tada   akenamashikaba
SKKS 13 (1205)

Why should I resent

a person's growing cold?

Time was

when he didn't know me

and I didn't know him either

·~·

Utoku naru   hito o nani tote   uramuran

shirarezu shiranu   ori mo arishi o

SKKS 14 (1297)

Cuckoo at the Time of Parting

At best of times,

hard to break away,

and now with the flush of dawn

cuckoo makes it worse

by singing out!*

·❧·

Saranu dani   kaeri yararenu   shinonome ni
soete katarau   hototogisu kana
SKS 2 (586)

* In Chinese and Japanese poetry, the cuckoo is the
bird of memory.

L o v e

Love Likened to Lemon Grass

Does this love of mine

face one way only,

never perversely straying?

Rather it is the lemon grass in the meadow,

tossed in ever-shifting winds

Hitokata ni   midaru tomo naki   waga koi ya
kaze sadamaranu   nobe no karukaya
SKS 2 (603)

Love

Her face when we parted,

a parting

I can never forget—

And for keepsake she left it

printed on the moon

Omokage no   wasuraru majiki   wakare kana
nagori o hito no   tsuki ni todomete
SKS 2 (621); SKKS 13 (1185)

L o v e

Does the moon say "Grieve!"

does it force

these thoughts on me?

And yet the tears come

to my reproving eyes

Nageke tote   tsuki ya wa mono o   omowasuru
kakochigao naru   waga namida kana
SKS 2 (628)

When the moon shines

without the smallest blemish,

I think of her—

and then my heart disfigures it,

blurs it with tears.

·～·

Kuma mo naki　orishimo hito o　omoiidete
kokoro to tsuki o　yatsushitsuru kana
SKS 2 (644), SKKS 14 (1268)

L o v e

When I gaze at it

these days,

lost in thoughts of love,

how deeply the moon's hue

seems dyed in sorrow

Mono omoite   nagamuru koro no   tsuki no iro ni
ikabakari naru   aware somuran
SKS 2 (649); SKKS 14 (1269)

As rays of moonlight stream

through a sudden gap

in the rain clouds —

if we could meet even

for so brief a moment!

·~·

Amagumo no   warinaki hima o   moru tsuki no
kage bakari dani   aimiteshi gana
SKS 2 (650)

L o v e

Now I understand—

when you said "Remember!"

and swore to do the same,

already you had it

in mind to forget

~

Kyō zo shiru   omoiideyo to   chigirishi wa
wasuren tote no   nasake narikeri
SKS 2 (685); SKKS 14 (1298)

L o v e

"I know

how you must feel!"

And with those words

she grows more hateful

than if she'd never spoken at all

Nakanaka ni   omoi shiru chō   koto no ha wa
towanu ni sugite   urameshiki kana
SKS 2 (688)

L o v e

My thoughts keep

growing lusher,

like summertime weeds,

though the sadness of autumn surfeit

I know lies ahead

·⌇·

Natsugusa no   shigeri no mi yuku   omoi kana
mataruru aki no   aware shirarete
SKS 2 (703)

L o v e

Why does no one say "Pitiful!"

or come to comfort me?

In the house

where I long for my love

the wind blows over the reeds

Aware tote   tou hito no nado   nakaruran
mono omou yado no   ogi no uwakaze
SKS 2 (705), SKKS 14 (1307)

MISCELLANEOUS

When I was in retirement in a distant place, I
sent this to someone in the capital around the
*time when there was a moon.**

Only the moon

high in the sky

as an empty reminder—

but if, looking at it, we just remember,

our two hearts may meet

.◡.

Tsuki nomi ya   uwa no sora naru   katami nite
omoi mo ideba   kokoro kayowan
SKS 2 (727); SKKS 14 (1267)

* In the *Shinkokinshū* this is included among the love
poems. Without knowing more about the identity of
the person addressed, however, it is impossible to say if
it deals with love or friendship.

When I abandoned the world and was on my way to Ise, I wrote this at Suzukayama (Bell Deer Mountain).*

Bell Deer Mountain:

I shake off this sad world,

put it aside,

but what lies in store for me,

what note will I sound?

Suzukayama   uki yo o yoso ni   furi sutete
ika ni nari yuku   waga mi naruran
SKS 2 (728); SKKS 17 (1611)

* Suzukayama is on the road between Kyoto and the Ise region, where Saigyō had friends. The poem was probably written not long after he entered religious life. The words *furi* (shake), *nari* (sound), and *naru* (to sound/ to become) are linked to the bell image in the name of the mountain.

Expressing Feelings

Is it because my mind

keeps dwelling

on every worldly thing

that the world seems

more hateful to me than ever?

·~·

Nanigoto ni   tomaru kokoro no   arikereba
sara ni shimo mata   yo no itowashiki
SKS 2 (729); SKKS 18 (1831)

*On my way to Tennō-ji I was rained on and
asked for lodging at a place called Eguchi. On
being refused, I wrote this.**

It's hard to despise

the whole world

as a borrowed lodging,

but that you should begrudge me

even one night's such lodging!

Yo no naka o   itou made koso   katakarame
kari no yadori o   oshimu kimi kana
SKS 2 (752); SKKS 10 (978)

* Tennō-ji is the Shitennō-ji temple in present-day
Osaka. Eguchi was a port on the Yodo River near Osaka
where travelers frequently stopped. It was famous for its
brothels.

Reply *

Because I heard you were someone

who had left the household life,

my only thought was to warn you:

don't let your mind dwell

on this borrowed lodging!

٠∾٠

Ie o izuru † 　 hito to shi kikeba 　 kari no yado
kokoro tomu na to 　 omou bakari zo
SKS 2 (753); SKKS 10 (979)

* in the SKKS, the writer of the reply is identified as a prostitute named Tae. The legend grew up that the reply to Saigyō's poem was written by one of the prostitutes at the house where he asked for lodging. She later became known as Eguchi no Kimi or The Lady of Eguchi and was regarded as a manifestation of the Bodhisattva Samandabhadra. The incident forms the basis of the Noh play "Eguchi."

† In the SKKS version of the poem, the opening phrase reads: Yo o itou, "someone who despises this world."

How have I spent

these many years and months

in this world

where those here even yesterday

are no longer here today?

Or, according to another interpretation:

Why have I been allotted

so many years and months

in this world

where those here even yesterday

are no longer here today?

·～·

Toshitsuki o   ika de waga mi ni   okuriken

kinō no hito mo   kyō wa naki yo ni

SKS 2 (768); SKKS 18 (1748)

Written when he was feeling very downcast and discouraged and heard a cricket singing close to his pillow.

At that time

on my pillow

under roots of mugwort,

then too may these insects

cheer me with friendly notes*

Sono ori no   yomogi ga moto no   makura ni mo
kaku koso mushi no   ne ni wa mutsureme
SKS 2 (775)

* Saigyō is imagining the time when he will be in his grave.

On the phrase "All Phenomena are Fleeting"*

I think of past times,

so swift

in their vanishing,

the present soon to follow—

dew on the morning-glory

Hakanakute   suginishi kata o   omou ni mo
ima mo sa koso wa   asagao no tsuyu
SKS 2 (777)

* From the famous verse in the seventh chapter of the
Nirvana Sutra: "All phenomena are fleeting, / this is the
law of birth and death. / When you have wiped out
birth and death, / nirvana is your joy."

Miscellaneous

When I was traveling in the province of Michinoku, I saw in the fields a grave
that seemed more imposing than ordinary. I asked someone and was told it was the
grave of the Middle Captain. I then asked who the Middle Captain might be, and
learned that it was Sanekata, which made me feel very sad. The scene was already
desolate enough, with pampas grass withered by frost dimly visible whichever way
one looked. And when I tried to describe it later, I felt as though words had failed
me.*

His name alone,

imperishable,

he left behind—

pampas grass in withered fields

I see as his memento

·〰·

Kuchi mo senu   sono na bakari   todome okite
kareno no susuki   katamini ni zo miru
SKS 2 (800); SKKS 8 (793)

* Fujiwara Sanekata, a captain in the imperial guard
and son of Fujiwara Sadatoki, was a distinguished poet
whose works are included in the *Shūishū* and other imperial anthologies. After quarreling with another member of the Fujiwara family in the palace, he was assigned
the post of governor of the province of Mutsu or Michinoku in the far north and died there in 998.

*After the Lady-in-Waiting of the Second Rank
to Taikemmon-in died, I wrote these ten poems
in company with others.**

On the waters

of the flowing river,

a jewel, a bead of foam—

the pity

of this fugitive world!

᠁

Nagare yuku   mizu ni tama nasu   utakata no
aware ada naru   kono yo narikeri
SKS 2 (817)

* The Lady-in-Waiting of the Second Rank was Fujiwara Asako, the second wife of the statesman Fujiwara
Michinori (d. 1159). She was wet nurse to Emperor
Go-Shirakawa and lady-in-waiting to Taikemmon-in,
the consort of Emperor Toba and mother of emperors
Sutoku and Go-Shirakawa. She died in the first month
of 1116. Saigyō, who had been a close friend of her
and her two sons, was forty-nine at the time.

*From "Ten Poems for the Lady-in-Waiting of
the Second Rank"*

We saw you off,

and returning through the fields

I thought the morning dew

had wet my sleeve,

but it was tears

Okuri okite   kaerishi nobe no   asa tsuyu o
sode ni utsusu wa   namida narikeri
SKS 2 (819)

*From "Ten Poems for the Lady-in-Waiting of
the Second Rank"*

Adding one more

to the graves

at the foot of Boat Hill,

we make you

"someone of the past"*

.~.

Funaoka no   susono no tsuka no   kazu soete
mukashi no hito ni   kimi o nashitsuru
SKS 2 (820)

* Funaoka or Boat Hill is a small hill in the northern
outskirts of Kyoto where bodies were cremated and
buried.

Miscellaneous

*From "Ten Poems for the Lady-in-Waiting of
the Second Rank"*

"Pray for me in

my life to come!"

she begged me promise—

those words a legacy

never to be forgot

⌁

Nochi no yo o   toe to chigirishi   koto no ha ya
wasuraru majiki   katami narubeki
SKS 2 (822)

*From "Ten Poems for the Lady-in-Waiting of
the Second Rank"*

The path we search for

in your wake

you've already entered,

never straying among

the bitter hills of death*

⸱ᴗ⸱

Ato o tou   michi ni ya kimi wa   irinuran
kurushiki shide no   yama e kakarade
SKS 2 (824)

* The "path" is the way of the Buddha; the lady-in-
waiting has already gone on to her next existence.

From "Poems on Impermanence"

Fishermen

by a rocky shore,

winds blowing wildly,

in a boat unmoored—

such is our condition!

⤳

Kaze araki   iso ni kakareru   amabito wa
tsunaganu fune no   kokochi koso sure
SKS 2 (846)

From "Poems on Impermanence"

Though whose remains lie here

I do not know,

Mount Toribe at sundown:

one by one

the terrible graves *

Naki ato o   tare to shiranedo   toribeyama
ono ono sugoki   tsuka no yūgure
SKS 2 (848)

* Mount Toribe is a hill east of Kyoto used as a cre-
matorium and graveyard.

Miscellaneous

From "Poems on Impermanence"

Rowing, rowing

through a world

where waves tower,

all of us tying up at last

at the foot of Boat Hill

Nami takaki   yo o kogi kogite   hito wa mina
funaoka yama o   tomari ni zo suru
SKS 2 (849)

*With others, writing on the theme "The Unde-
termined Nature of the Inborn Mind"* *

Like star lilies

that sway in thick-grown fields

where larks fly up,

this mind bound

to no one thing

・～・

Hibari tatsu   arano ni ouru   himeyuri no
nani ni tsuku to mo   naki kokoro kana
SKS 2 (866)

* The innate mind has the potential to achieve various
states of enlightenment, a fact symbolized by the sway-
ing blossoms of the lilies. There is a play on *yuri*/lily
and *yuri*/wavering.

Reciting the Buddha's Name at Dawn

In rhythm with

the tolling of the bell

that wakens us from dreams,

ten times I intone

the sacred name

·~·

Yume samuru   kane no hibiki ni   uchisoete
totabi no mina o   tonaetsuru kana
SKS 2 (871)

Meditation on the Mind

Darkness dispelled,

is the radiant moon that dwells

in the skies of the mind

drawing nearer now

to western hilltops?*

·~·

Yami harete   kokoro no sora ni   sumu tsuki wa
nishi no yamabe ya   chikaku naruran
SKS 2 (876); SKKS 20 (1979)

* West is the direction of death and of the Western
Paradise of the Buddha Amida.

Sent from Mount Kōya to someone in the capital*

Clarity of mind comes

from one's surroundings,

I tell myself,

but this mountaintop where I live

is a cheerless place!

·ᵥ·

Sumu koto wa   tokorogara zo to   iinagara
takano wa mono no   aware naru kana
SKS 2 (913)

* According to one theory, the "someone" is the poet's
wife, whom he left when he entered religious life.

In this mountain village

where I've given up

all hope of visitors,

how drab life would be

without my loneliness

Tou hito mo   omoi taetaru   yamazato no
sabishisa nakuba   sumi ukaramashi
SKS 2 (937)

The twilight bell

I waited for

is sounding—

if tomorrow is granted me,

I'll listen for it again*

·～·

Mataretsuru   iriai no kane no   oto su nari
asu mo ya araba   kikan to suran
SKS 2 (939); SKKS 18 (1808)

* The *iriai no kane* or twilight bell is sounded at most temples at the close of day. Its striking reminds one of the closing of a lifetime and the evanescence of the world.

Mountain village

where wind makes sad noises

in the pines—

and adding to the loneliness,

the cry of an evening cicada

Matsukaze no   oto aware naru   yamazato ni

sabishisa souru   higurashi no koe

SKS 2 (940)

A single pine tree

growing in the hollow—

and I thought

I was the only one

without a friend

·~·

Tani no ma ni   hitori zo matsu mo   taterikeru
ware nomi tomo wa   naki ka to omoeba
SKS 2 (941)

I don't know

what's beyond the mountain

where the late sunlight streams,

but already I've sent

my mind on ahead*

.⌣.

Irihi sasu   yama no anata wa   shiranedomo
kokoro o kanete   okuri okitsuru
SKS 2 (942)

* The mountain of the setting sun symbolizes the
Western Pardise of Amida Buddha.

The sound of water

is my companion

in this lonely hut

in lulls between

the storms on the peak

·⤙·

Mizu no oto wa   sabishiki io no   tomo nare ya

mine no arashi no   taema taema ni

SKS 2 (944)

In reaped fields

where quail cry,

rice stubble puts up new shoots,

rays of a crescent moon

lighting them dimly

Uzura naku   karita no hitsuji   oi idete
honoka ni terasu   mikazuki no kage
SKS 2 (945)

In this lodging

that no one visits,

where no one comes to call,

from the moon in the trees

beams of light come poking in

.~.

Tazune kite   kototou hito no   naki yado ni
ko no ma no tsuki no   kage zo sashi kuru
SKS 2 (949)

In a hailstorm

you can hear

they're there all right—

the dried leaves fallen

from the twigs of the oaks

·∖·

Arare ni zo   monomekashiku wa   kikoekeru
karetaru nara no   shiba no ochiba wa*
SKS 2 (964)

* For the first phrase I follow the reading in the *Rokka-shū* text. The Yomei bunko text reads *Aware ni zo*, which yields the translation:

  Mournful,
  with a sharp sound,
  you hear them—
  the dried leaves falling
  from the twigs of the oaks

1 5 2

On a little ridge

of evergreens

where two rivers meet,

woodsmen on the rocks—

how cool they must be!

·◡·

Kawaai ya   maki no susoyama   ishi tatete
somabito ika ni   suzushikaruran
SKS 2 (974)

In a tree that stands

on the crag

by abandoned paddies,

a dove calling to its companion

in the desolate twilight

Furuhata no   soba no tatsu ki ni   iru hato no
tomo yobu koe no   sugoki yūgure
SKS 2 (997), SKKS 17 (1674)

Butterflies darting

so familiarly among the flowers

that bloom by the fence—

I envy them, yet know

how little time they have left

Mase ni saku   hana ni mutsurete   tobu chō no
urayamashiku mo   hakanakarikeri
SKS 2 (1026)

Cherry petals,

like the tears

of someone who's lonely,

showering down

when the wind blows cold

.~.

Wabibito no   namida ni nitaru   sakura kana
kaze mi ni shimeba   mazu koboretsutsu
SKS 2 (1035)

Mount Yoshino—

I doubt

I'll be leaving it soon,

though friends I'm sure are waiting,

saying, "Once the blossoms have fallen—"

·~·

Yoshinoyama   yagate ideji to   omou mi o
hana chiranaba to   hito ya matsuran
SKS 2 (1036), SKKS 17 (1617)

Were we sure of seeing

a moon like this

in existences to come,

who would be sorry

to leave this life?

·∽·

Kon yo ni mo   kakaru tsuki o shi   mirubekuba
inochi o oshimu   hito nakaramashi
SKS 2 (1040)

Poem written when parting from a friend going to the province of Michinoku*

And when you're gone

I'll keep on gazing,

as though waiting for the moon,

gazing eastward

at the evening sky

Kimi inaba   tsuki matsu tote mo   nagame yaran
azuma no kata no   yūgure no sora
SKS 3 (1046); SKKS 9 (885)

* In far northeastern Japan

*On Mount Kōya, writing with others on the
theme "Late Night, the Sound of Water"*

The storm at the window

has ceased its roaring,

and the sound of water,

lost in the din before,

tells us night is far gone

.〜.

Magiretsuru   mado no arashi no   koe tomete
fukuru o tsuguru   mizu no oto kana
SKS 3 (1049)

In the bright light of the spring moon, looking
at branches of cherry that haven't yet begun to
blossom as they sway in the wind.

Looking at the moon,

I see the branches of cherry

trembling in the wind

and almost tell myself,

"They're in bloom!"

Tsuki mireba   kaze ni sakura no   eda naete
hana yo tsuguru   kokochi koso sure
SKS 3 (1069)

Once long ago, when I was on my way to Mount Shosha in Harima, I came on a pool of clear water in the midst of a meadow. Some years later, I happened to pass by the spot in the course of religious practice and found it looking as it had before, quite unchanged.*

Clear waters unchanged

in a meadow

I saw once long ago,

will you remember

this face of mine?

·〜·

Mukashi mishi   nonaka no shimizu   kawaraneba

waga kage o mo ya   omoi izuran

SKS 3 (1096)

* Mount Shosha, near the city of Himeji in Hyogo Prefecture, is the site of Enkyō-ji, one of the most important temples of the Tendai sect of Buddhism.

Writing a poem on travel

Parting me

from the capital,

these mountains I've crossed—

now even they

are fading into the mist!

⸱⟋⸱

Koe kitsuru   miyako hedatsuru   yama sae ni

hate wa kasumi ni   kienu meru kana

SKS 3 (1100)

We'll look at the moon

and remember!—

so we vowed when I left.

Tonight someone at home too

must be wetting a sleeve with tears.

Tsuki miba to   chigirite ideshi   furusato no
hito mo ya koyoi   sode nurasuran
SKKS 10 (938)

I paid reverence to the Three-Tiered Waterfall.
It was particularly awesome and I felt that all
my sins of the three types of karma must be
*wiped away.**

Heaped on my body,

sins of words too

are washed away,

my mind made spotless

by the Three-Tiered Waterfall†

·↘·

Mi ni tsumoru   kotoba no tsumi mo   arawarete
kokoro suminuru   mikasane no taki
SKS 3 (1118)

* The poem is one of a series describing a pilgrimage
to holy places at Mount Ōmine in present-day Nara
Prefecture. The three types of karma are actions of the
body, mouth, and mind.

† By "sins of words" Saigyō may simply mean words
spoken in anger or unwisely, though it is possible that,
like many poets who were also devout Buddhist believ-
ers, he felt that his literary activities were to some
degree in conflict with his religious goals.

The loneliness

of my ramshackle

grass hut,

where no one but the wind

comes to call

.∼.

Abaretaru   kusa no iori no   sabishisa wa
kaze yori hoka ni   tou hito zo naki
SKS 3 (1148)

With others, writing on the theme "In Tree Shade, Enjoying the Cool"

Today again

I'll go to the hill

where pine winds blow—

perhaps to meet my friend

who was cooling himself there yesterday

Kyō mo mata   matsu no kaze fuku   oka e yukan
kinō suzumishi   tomo ni au ya to
SKS 3 (1152)

After the last light of the setting sun had vanished,
the moon shone in my window

Replacing the rays

of late sun

that streamed in the window,

shedding a different light:

an early evening moon

·~·

Sashikitsuru   mado no irihi o   aratamete
hikari o kauru   yūzukuyo kana

SKS 3 (1153)

*The Lay Priest Jakunen is living in Ōhara. I
sent him these from Mount Kōya.**

So remote the mountains,

the only callers to break

the tedium of my window

are top branches of sumac

just starting to change color

·⌇·

Yama fukami   mado no tsurezure   tou mono wa
irozuki somuru   haji no tachieda
SKS 3 (1200)

* Saigyō sent a set of ten poems to his old friend
Jakunen (Fujiwara Yorinari), who was living in religious
retirement at Ōhara, a village north of Kyoto. The
poems all begin with the same phrase, *Yama fukami*, and
describe Saigyō's retreat at Mount Kōya. These are the
third, fourth, fifth, sixth, eighth, and tenth in the series.

So remote the mountains,

on a carpet of moss

a monkey sits,

unconcernedly

chattering

꒰ ꒱

Yama fukami   koke no mushiro no   ue ni ite
nanigokoro naku   naku mashira kana
SKS 3 (1201)

So remote the mountains,

I collect water

as it drips from the rocks,

in intervals gathering horse chestnuts

that come plop-plopping down*

⌒·

Yama fukami   iwa ni shidaruru   mizu tamen
katsugatsu otsuru   tochi hirou hodo
SKS 3 (1202)

* The horse chestnuts are pounded into meal and used
for food.

So remote the mountains,

no friendly birds

chirping close by—

only the fearful

voice of the owl

Yama fukami   kejikaki tori no   oto wa sede
monoosoroshiki   fukurō no koe

SKS 3 (1203)

So remote the mountains—

then I hear somone

chopping brush for kindling,

the noise of the ax

raising a clatter

⁓

Yama fukami   hota kiru nari to   kikoetsutsu
tokoro nigiwau   ono no oto kana
SKS 3 (1205)

So remote the mountains,

deer fearless enough

to come right up close

tell me how far I am

from the outside world!

·~·

Yama fukami   naruru kasegi no   kejikasa ni
yo ni tōzakaru   hodo zo shiraruru
SKS 3 (1207)

Miscellaneous

From "One Hundred and Ten Love Poems"

Though it reaches

deep into the heart,

the fragrance is meaningless

while the sprig of plum

remains unplucked

Kokoro ni wa   fukaku shimedomo   mume no hana
oranu nioi wa   kai nakarikeri
SKS 3 (1255)

From "One Hundred and Ten Love Poems"

Keen to the danger,

constantly I shun

the eyes of others,

treading like one on a plank trail

rigged across the face of the cliff

·〜·

Ayausa ni   hitome zo tsune ni   yogarekeru
iwa no kado fumu   hoki no kakemichi
SKS 3 (1333)

Miscellaneous

From "One Hundred and Ten Love Poems"

As the leaves

of the kudzu vine,

no longer cupping dew,

turn about in the buffeting wind,

turn your thoughts to me!

·～·

Fuku kaze in   tsuyu mo tamaranu   kuzu no ha no
uragaere to wa   kimi o koso omoe
SKS 3 (1335)

From "One Hundred and Ten Love Poems"

My love will end

in hopelessness—

these longing sighs

I bring on myself

are empty as the cicada's shell

Munashikute yaminubeki kana utsusemi no

kono mi kara nite omou nageki wa

SKS 3 (1337)

From "One Hundred and Ten Love Poems"

However looked at,

it's a world

to be loathed—

but as long as you live there

I'm drawn to it!

·∼·

Tonikaku ni   itowamahoshiki   yo naredomo
kimi ga sumu ni mo   hikarenuru kana
SKS 3 (1348)

Miscellaneous

From "One Hundred and Ten Love Poems"

What else

could have made me

loathe the world?

The one who was cruel to me

today I think of as kind*

Nanigoto ni   tsukete ka yo o ba   itowamashi
ukarishi hito zo   kyō wa ureshiki
SKS 3 (1349)

* This and the preceding poem are sometimes cited as
evidence that Saigyō entered religious life because of a
disappointment in love.

*I made a journey to Sanuki, and at a place
called the port of Matsuyama, searched for the
spot where the Retired Emperor resided, but
could find no trace of it.**

That ship that came,

washed on the waves

of Matsuyama,

in no time vanished

into nothingness!

·～·

Matsuyama no   nami ni nagarete   koshi fune no
yagate munashiku   narinikeru kana
SKS 3 (1353)

* In 1167 or 1168 Saigyō journeyed to the province of
Sanuki in Shikoku to pay respects to the memory of
Emperor Sutoku (r. 1124–1141), who was banished to
Sanuki in 1156 as a result of his part in the Hōgen civil
war. He died there in 1164.

The waves

of Matsuyama—

their aspect is unchanged,

but of you, my lord,

no trace remains

———

Matsuyama no   nami no keshiki wa   kawaraji o
kata naku kimi wa   narimashinikeri
SKS 3 (1354)

*In the same province, on the mountain near the
place where the Daishi lived, I built a hut and
lived in it. I wrote this when the moon was
exceptionally bright and I looked out at the
cloudless sea.**

I look out

from the cloudless mountain

at moonlight on the sea,

its islands so many rents

in a sheet of ice

٠ﹶ٠

Kumori naki   yama nite umi no   tsuki mireba

shima zo kōri no   taema narikeru

SKS 3 (1356)

* Written on Saigyō's journey to Sanuki. He was stay-
ing at Zentsū-ji, a temple located at the birthplace of
Kōbō Daishi or Kūkai (774–835), the founder of the
Shingon sect of Buddhism in Japan.

*On looking at the pine that stands in front
of my hut*

Live through the long years,

pine, and pray for me

in my next existence,

I who'll have no one

to visit the places I once was*

⌖

Hisa ni hete   waga nochi no yo o   toeyo matsu
ato shinobubeki   hito mo naki mi zo
SKS 3 (1358)

---

* As Saigyō is now visiting the site of Kōbō Daishi's
birth.

When I tire of this spot as well,

too gloomy to live in,

when I drift

on my way, pine,

you'll be left alone

˙˯˙

Koko o mata   ware sumiukute   ukarenaba
matsu wa hitori ni   naran to suran
SKS 3 (1359)

On a snowfall *

Under the pines,

a color like the sky

when snow falls,

the rest of the mountain trail

one swath of white cloth

·➤·

Matsu no shita wa   yuki furu ori no   iro nare ya

mina shirotae ni   miyuru yamaji ni

SKS 3 (1360)

---

* This and the following poem were written when Saigyō was living in retreat in a hut at Zentsū-ji.

How timely

the delight of

this snowfall,

obliterating the mountain trail

just when I wanted to be alone!

·～·

Orishimo are   ureshiku yuki no   uzumu kana
kakikomorinan to   omou yamaji o
SKS 3 (1364)

*Observing divers coming and going in Ushimado
Channel, gathering turban shells and loading
them in boats**

In a channel

where turban shells live,

the sight of divers busily

hunting them

in the hollows of the rock

⋅❧⋅

Sadae sumu   seto no iwatsubo   motome idete
isogishi ama no   keshiki naru kana
SKS 3 (1376)

* Ushimado is on the Inland Sea in Okayama Prefecture

The float-rigged strands

of the nets

that catch little bream

seem to be moving shoreward—

sad work in Shiozaki Bay*

.⌣.

Kotai hiku   ami no ukenawa   yorikumeri
uki shiwaza aru   shiozaki no ura
SKS 3 (1378)

* Shiozaki Bay is on the southwest coast of Awaji Island in the Inland Sea. Here, and elsewhere, Saigyō
deplores occupations such as hunting and fishing that
involve the taking of life, since they create bad karma
for the persons engaged in them.

Fishermen home from

their day's work:

on a bed of seaweed,

little top shells, clams,

hermit crabs, periwinkles

Amabito no   isoshiku kaeru   hijiki mono wa
konishi hamaguri   gōna shitadami
SKS 3 (1380)

When I crossed over to Irago, I found clam-like shells called mussels that often bear pearls. I wrote this on observing the towering piles of shells from which such pearls had been extracted.*

Pearls plucked,

the mussel shells

lie heaped in mounds,

showing us

the aftermath of treasure

⸱∿⸱

Akoya toru   igai no kara o   tsumi okite

takara no ato o   misuru narikeri

SKS 3 (1387)

---

* Irago is a peninsula south of Nagoya in Aichi. Saigyō had crossed over from the nearby Shima peninsula in Mie Prefecture.

A strong wind came up from the offing and the
boats that fish for bonito returned to port

Side by side

the bonito boats approach

the cape of Irago,

bobbing on the waves

of the northwest wind

Iragozaki no   katsuo tsuribune   narabi ukite
hagachi no nami ni   ukabitsutsu zo yoru
SKS 3 (1388)

Poems on small birds

If they didn't sing

we'd just take them

for deeper-hued leaves—

the flocks of greenfinches

feeding on willow buds

Koe sezuba   iro koku naru to   omowamashi
yanagi no me hamu   hiwa no muradori
SKS 3 (1399)

Poems on small birds

Lined up,

never leaving their companions,

the willow tits

count on the lower limbs

of the pasania for their roost

·∼·

Narabi ite   tomo o hanarenu   kogarame no
negura ni tanomu   shii no shitaeda
SKS 3 (1401)

Written on a moonlit night when visiting Kamo*

In the bed of the Mioya River,

flooded in clear moonlight,

the frost is cold.

I hear plovers crying

as they fly far off

·≺·

Tsuki no sumu   mioyagawara ni   shimo saete
chidori tōdatsu   koe kikoyu nari
SKS 3 (1402)

---

* The Shimogamo Shrine in Kyoto; the Mioya River is probably the small Tadasu River that runs through the grounds of the shrine, though it perhaps indicates the much larger Kamo River nearby.

Miscellaneous

*Traveling in the province of Sanuki, I arrived
at a port called Minotsu. The moon was bright
and the fishermen's frames* could be seen as far
out in the water as they could be erected. Sea
birds were flying all around the poles that hold
the frames in place.*

Sheath of spreading

moonlight one would

almost take for ice,

flocks of teal circling

the poles of the fishermen's frames

·◡·

Shikiwatasu   tsuki no kōri o   utagaite
hibi no te mawaru   aji no muradori
SKS 3 (1404)

* Rough frames of bamboo erected for catching fish or
raising oysters or edible seaweed.

I have cast off the world

but there are thoughts

I cannot cast away—

I who have yet

to part from the capital

Yo no naka o   sutete suteenu   kokochi shite
miyako hanarenu   waga mi narikeri
SKS 3 (1417)

Who would remember,

who would come

looking for me,

pushing his way along this mountain path

so drenched in dew?

.⌒.

Omoi idete   tare ka wa tomete   wake mo kon
iru yamamichi no   tsuyu no fukasa o
SKS 3 (1427)

*From "One Hundred Poems: Ten Poems Ex-
pressing Feelings"*

Time to say goodby

to such glories—

thoughts of them end now—

to long familiar blossoms

on the peak of the immortals*

·〜·

Iza saraba   sakari omou mo   hodo mo araji
hakoya ga mine no   hana ni mutsureshi
SKS 3 (1503)

* The "peak of the immortals" is believed to be a refer-
ence to the retired emperor's palace and the poem to
express Saigyō's determination to leave the service of
the Retired Emperor Toba and enter religious life.

From "One Hundred Poems: Ten Poems on
Impermanence"

Drops of dew

strung on filaments

of spider web—

such are the trappings

that deck out this world

⸱⸰⸱

Sasagani no   ito ni tsuranuku   tsuyu no tama o
kakete kazareru   yo ni koso arikere
SKS 3 (1514)

From "One Hundred Poems: Ten Poems on Impermanence"

Since I no longer think

of reality

as reality,

what reason would I have

to think of dreams as dreams?

·❧·

Utsutsu o mo   utsutsu to sara ni   omoeneba
yume o mo yume to   nani ka omowan
SKS 3 (1515)

From "One Hundred Poems: Ten Poems on
Impermanence"

The great net

has been hauled in

close to shore —

how many living things

are tangled in its meshes?

⌇

Migiwa chikaku   hikiyoseraruru   ōami ni
ikuse no mono no   inochi komoreri
SKS 3 (1519)

From *"One Hundred Poems: Ten Poems on Impermanence"*

Is it time now

for peaceful death?

Accept the thought

and at once

the mind replies, "Oh yes!"

·⌒·

Uraura to   shinanzuru na to   omoi tokeba

kokoro no yagate   sa zo to kotauru

SKS 3 (1520)

From "One Hundred Poems: Ten Poems on
Buddhism"

Would the flames of thought

that envelop your body

ever be quenched?

Never but for the blowing

of these cool winds!*

·ᴖ·

Mi ni tsukite   moyuru omoi no   kiemashi ya
suzushiki kaze no   augazariseba
SKS 3 (1538)

* The winds are the Buddha's teachings, particularly as
set forth in the *Lotus Sutra*. The poem is one of three on
the *Muryōgikyō* or *Sutra of Immeasurable Meanings*, which is
often treated as an introduction to the *Lotus Sutra*.

From "One Hundred Poems: Ten Miscellaneous Poems"

In a mountain village

when I'm lost in the dark

of the mind's dreaming,

the sound of the wind

blows me to brightness

.~.

Yamazato no   kokoro no yume ni   madoi oreba
fuki shiramakasu   kaze no oto kana
SKS 3 (1549)

*From "One Hundred Poems: Ten Miscellaneous
Poems"*

Gazing at the moon,

yes—then my mind

drifts wholly away from me,

but why does it wander

even when skies are black?

Tsuki o koso   nagameba kokoro   ukare ideme

yami naru sora ni   tadayou ya nazo

SKS 3 (1550)

When you consider,

all in this world

are blossoms that fall—

and this body of mine,

where will I lay it down?

Yo no naka o   omoeba nabete   chiru hana no
waga mi o sate mo   izuchi ka mo sen
SKKS 16 (1470)

If I've truly renounced it,

I should show how I abhor

this troubled world—

for my sake, cloud over,

moon of the autumn night!

·~·

Sutsu to naraba   uki yo o itou   shirushi aran
ware ni wa kumore   aki no yo no tsuki
SKKS 16 (1533)

Miscellaneous

Written on a journey to the eastern provinces

Did I ever think

in old age

I would cross it again?

So long I've lived,

Saya-between-the-Hills *

Toshi takete   mata koyubeshi to   omoiki ya
inochi narikeri   saya no nakayama
SKKS 10 (987)

* A long winding road over the mountains in present-
day Shizuoka Prefecture. The poem was written on
Saigyō's second journey to Michinoku, when he was
nearing seventy.

*On Mt. Fuji, written when carrying out religious
practice in the eastern provinces.*

Trailing on the wind,

the smoke of Mount Fuji

fades in the sky,

moving like my thoughts

toward some unknown end

·ᴗ·

Kaze ni nabiku   fuji no keburi no   sora ni kiete
yukue mo shiranu   waga omoi kana
SKKS 17 (1613)

Though in mind

you may journey easily

into the depths of the mountains,

without living here

how can you know their loneliness?

·~·

Yama fukaku   sa koso kokoro wa   kayou to mo
sumade aware o   shiran mono ka wa
SKKS 17 (1630)

Who lives there,

learning such loneliness?—

mountain village

where rains drench down

from an evening sky

·╲·

Tare sumite   aware shiruran   yamazato no

ame furisusan   yūgure no sora

SKKS 17 (1640)

Miscellaneous

Hearing that someone was embarking on an unthinkable course, I sent this from Mount Kōya to the person of whom it was reported.

Not stopping to mark the trail,

let me push even deeper

into the mountain!

Perhaps there's a place

where bad news can never reach me!*

.᠊᠊.

Shiori seji   nao yama fukaku   wakeiran
uki koto kikanu   tokoro ari ya to
SKS 3 (1121); SKKS 17 (1641)

* There is no way to determine the exact nature of the distressing report that reached Saigyō and the background of the poem remains a riddle.

A seedling pine in the garden

when I saw it long ago —

years have gone by

and now I hear the storm winds

roaring in its topmost branches

Mukashi mishi　niwa no komatsu ni　toshi furite
arashi no oto o　kozue ni zo kiku
SKKS 17 (1677)

Could this be it—

the spot where I lived

long ago?

Moonlight glitters

in the dew on the mugwort

·~·

Kore ya mishi   mukashi sumiken   ato naran
yomogi ga tsuyu ni   tsuki no kakareru
SKKS 17 (1680)

If I can find

no place fit to live,

let me live "no place"—

in this hut of sticks

flimsy as the world itself

.‿.

Izuku ni mo   sumarezuba tada   sumade aran
shiba no iori no   shibashi naru yo ni*
SKKS 18 (1778)

* In the last two lines of the original there is a play on
the words *shiba*, "sticks" or "brushwood," the material
from which the recluse's hut is made, and *shibashi*, "fleeting," which can apply both to the hut and to the world
as a whole.

My mind I send

with the moon

that goes beyond the mountain,

but what of this body

left behind in darkness?*

.~.

Tsuki no yuku   yama ni kokoro o   okuri irete
yami naru ato no   mi o ika ni sen
SKKS 18 (1779)

* The mountain here stands for the Western Paradise
of Amida Buddha.

Miscellaneous

When the priest Jakuren urged people to join him in composing hundred-poem sequences, I declined to participate. But while I was on my way on a pilgrimage to Kumano, I had a dream in which the bettō *Tankai appeared and said to Shunzei, "Though all other things may decline, the Way of Japanese poetry alone continues without change even in this latter age. One should compose poems as requested." After I awoke from the dream, I hastily composed the set of a hundred poems earlier requested and sent it to Jakuren. As a postscript I added this poem.**

Even in a latter age

this art alone

remains unchanged!

But had I not had that dream,

I'd have thought it none of my affair

·~·

Sue no yo mo   kono nasake no mi   kawarazu to
mishi yume nakuba   yoso ni kikamashi
SKKS 18 (1844)

---

* Priest Jakuren is Fujiwara Sadanaga (d. 1202). Tankai, an old friend of Saigyō, was the eighteenth *bettō* or administrator of the Kumano Shrine in the Kii peninsula to which Saigyō was making his pilgrimage. He had probably been dead several years at the time of the dream. Shunzei is the famous poet Fujiwara Shunzei (1114–1204), a close friend of Saigyō.

He who casts himself away—

has he truly

cast himself away?

The real castaway is one

who casts nothing away at all!*

Mi o sutsuru   hito wa makoto ni   sutsuru ka wa
sutenu hito koso   sutsuru narikere
Shikashū 10 (371)

* By "casting oneself away," Saigyō means renouncing
one's position in secular society and entering religious
life. A variant of the first line reads *Yo o sutsuru*, "He
who casts off the world."

Miscellaneous

*In the reign of Emperor Takakura (1171–1179),
I had occasion to submit a memorial to the
throne and appended this poem to it.**

Let us seek the past,

be an age

that cherishes the old—

then our "today" one day

will be someone's "long ago"

⸱⸜⸱

Ato tomete   furuki o shitau   yo naranan
ima mo arieba   mukashi   narubeshi
Shinchokusenshū ch. 17

---

* We do not know what Saigyō's memorial was about,
though perhaps it concerned one of the imperial anthologies. The poem, which is preserved in the *Shinchokusenshū*, an imperial anthology completed around 1234,
appears to represent Saigyō's statement on poetics: Look
to the past, for only then can your work serve as a
model for the future.

Miscellaneous

Composed when visiting the Tsukiyomi Shrine in
Ise and viewing the moon

Shining from the sky

over the tall peak

of Eagle Mountain,

the groves of Tsukiyomi

filtering, softening its rays*

·⌣·

Sayaka naru washi no takane no kumoi yori
kage yawaraguru tsukiyomi no mori
SKKS 19 (1879)

* The moon shining in the poem stands for Shakyamuni Buddha, who preached the *Lotus Sutra* at Eagle
Mountain in India. The supreme and universally valid
wisdom of the Buddha is "filtered" and adapted to local
spiritual needs through the person of the Japanese Shinto
deity Tsukiyomi, the goddess of the moon.

POEMS FROM THE

KIKIGAKISHŪ

*When I was living in Saga, I and others wrote poems in a light vein**

Startled by the sound

of children blowing wildly

on straw whistles,

I wake from my summer

noonday nap

⌒·

Unaigo ga   susami ni narasu   mugibue no
koe ni odoroku   natsu no hirufushi
Kikigaki shū

* A series of thirteen poems written by Saigyō some-
time in his late years. They are unusually colloquial in
tone. The following are the first, third, fourth, fifth,
sixth, tenth, and thirteenth in the series.

From the series of thirteen poems "in a light vein"

Not for stilts

but as a cane

bamboo serves me now,

I who call to mind

the games of childhood *

Takeuma o tsue ni mo kyō wa tanomu kana
warawa asobi o omoi idetsutsu

Kikigaki shū

* Children used partially split stalks of bamboo as stilts.

From the series of thirteen poems "in a light vein"

Just to play

hide and seek

the way I did long ago—

crouched down in a corner,

squeezing in so tight

·~·

Mukashi seshi   kakure asobi ni   narinaba ya
kata sumi moto ni   yori fuseritsutsu
Kikigaki shū

Poems from the Kikigaki shū

From the series of thirteen poems "in a light vein"

Drawing his

sparrow-hunting bow

of bent bamboo,

the little boy seems to be wishing

for a guardsman's black hat

᠊᠊᠊

Shino tamete   suzume yumi haru   o no warawa
hitai eboshi no   hoshige naru kana
Kikigaki shū

Poems from the Kikigaki shū

*From the series of thirteen poems "in a light
vein"*

I too

grew up the same way,

passing the years

playing games like them

in the garden sand

.·.

Ware mo sazo   niwa no isago no   tsuchi asobi
sate oitateru   mi ni koso arikere
Kikigaki shū

*From the series of thirteen poems "in a light
vein"*

My love was real,

yet treated as a joke —

in that long ago

childhood,

how I felt it!*

ᘛ

Koishiki o   tawaburerareshi   sono kami no
iwakenakarishi   ori no kokoro wa

Kikigaki shū

---

* Saigyō is apparently recalling some childhood infat-
uation that was dismissed lightly by the other party.

Poems from the Kikigaki shū

From the series of thirteen poems "in a light vein"

Overgrown with water shield,

sunk in the pond,

the upright stone

no longer upright

by the water's edge*

·～·

Nunawa hau   ike ni shizumeru   tateishi no
tatetaru koto mo   naki migiwa kana
Kikigaki Shū

* The "upright stone no longer upright" presumably conveys some kind of allegorical meaning.

Poems from the Kikigaki shū

From the series "Looking at pictures of hell"

Hard as it is

to be born a human being,

having risen this high,

who could fail to take warning,

sink down again!*

∿

Ukegataki   hito no sugata ni   ukami idete
korizu ya tare mo   mata shizumubeki

Kikigaki shū, SKKS 18 (1749)

* Ordinary unenlightened beings are believed to be
subject to rebirth in one of six realms which, in ascend-
ing order, are those of hell, hungry spirits, animals,
asuras, human beings, and heavenly beings. The deeds
one has done in previous lives determine which realm
one will be reborn in. The human realm, being next to
the highest, is difficult to be born in, but in it one may
hear the teachings of Buddhism and learn not to commit
the kind of evil deeds that will condemn one to rebirth
in the lower realms.

Poems from the Kikigaki shū

From the series "Looking at pictures of hell"

Did I hear you ask

what the fires of hell

are burning for?

They burn away evil

and the firewood is you!

‵‿‵

Tou to ka ya   nani yue moyuru   homura zo to
kimi o takigi no   tsumi no hi zo kashi
Kikigaki shū

Other Works
in the
Columbia Asian Studies Series

TRANSLATIONS FROM THE ORIENTAL CLASSICS

Major Plays of Chikamatsu, tr. Donald Keene   1961
Four Major Plays of Chikamatsu, tr. Donald Keene. Paperback
    text edition   1961
*Records of the Grand Historian of China, translated from the Shih chi
    of Ssu-ma Ch'ien*, tr. Burton Watson, 2 vols.   1961
*Instructions for Practical Living and Other Neo-Confucian Writings
    by Wang Yang-ming*, tr. Wing-tsit Chan   1963
Chuang Tzu: Basic Writings, tr. Burton Watson, paperback ed.
    only   1964
The Mahābhārata, tr. Chakravarthi V. Narasimhan. Also in
    paperback ed.   1965
The Manyōshū, Nippon Gakujutsu Shinkōkai edition   1965
Su Tung-p'o: Selections from a Sung Dynasty Poet, tr. Burton
    Watson. Also in paperback ed.   1965
Bhartrihari: Poems, tr. Barbara Stoler Miller. Also in paperback
    ed.   1967
Basic Writings of Mo Tzu, Hsün Tzu, and Han Fei Tzu, tr. Burton
    Watson. Also in separate paperback eds.   1967
The Awakening of Faith, Attributed to Aśvaghosha, tr. Yoshito S.
    Hakeda. Also in paperback ed.   1967
Reflections on Things at Hand: The Neo-Confucian Anthology, comp.
    Chu Hsi and Lü Tsu-ch'ien, tr. Wing-tsit Chan   1967
The Platform Sutra of the Sixth Patriarch, tr. Philip B. Yampolsky.
    Also in paperback ed.   1967
Essays in Idleness: The Tsurezuregusa of Kenkō, tr. Donald Keene.
    Also in paperback ed.   1967
The Pillow Book of Sei Shōnagon, tr. Ivan Morris, 2 vols.   1967
*Two Plays of Ancient India: The Little Clay Cart and the Minister's
    Seal*, tr. J. A. B. van Buitenen   1968
The Complete Works of Chuang Tzu, tr. Burton Watson   1968

The Romance of the Western Chamber (Hsi Hsiang chi), tr. S. I.
Hsiung. Also in paperback ed.   1968
The Manyōshū, Nippon Gakujutsu Shinkōkai edition.
Paperback text edition.   1969
Records of the Historian: Chapters from the Shih chi of Ssu-ma Ch'ien.
Paperback text edition, tr. Burton Watson.   1969
Cold Mountain: 100 Poems by the T'ang Poet Han-shan, tr. Burton
Watson. Also in paperback ed.   1970
Twenty Plays of the Nō Theatre, ed. Donald Keene. Also in
paperback ed.   1970
Chūshingura: The Treasury of Loyal Retainers, tr. Donald Keene.
Also in paperback ed.   1971
The Zen Master Hakuin: Selected Writings, tr. Philip B. Yampolsky   1971
Chinese Rhyme-Prose: Poems in the Fu Form from the Han and Six
Dynasties Periods, tr. Burton Watson. Also in paperback
ed.   1971
Kūkai: Major Works, tr. Yoshito S. Hakeda. Also in paperback
ed.   1972
The Old Man Who Does as He Pleases: Selections from the Poetry
and Prose of Lu Yu, tr. Burton Watson   1973
The Lion's Roar of Queen Śrīmālā, tr. Alex and Hideko Wayman   1974
Courtier and Commoner in Ancient China: Selections from the History
of the Former Han by Pan Ku, tr. Burton Watson. Also in
paperback ed.   1974
Japanese Literature in Chinese, vol. 1: Poetry and Prose in Chinese
by Japanese Writers of the Early Period, tr. Burton Watson   1975
Japanese Literature in Chinese, vol. 2: Poetry and Prose in Chinese
by Japanese Writers of the Later Period, tr. Burton Watson   1976
Scripture of the Lotus Blossom of the Fine Dharma, tr. Leon Hurvitz.
Also in paperback ed.   1976
Love Song of the Dark Lord: Jayadeva's Gītagovinda, tr. Barbara
Stoler Miller. Also in paperback ed. Cloth ed. includes
critical text of the Sanskrit.   1977
Ryōkan: Zen Monk-Poet of Japan, tr. Burton Watson   1977
Calming the Mind and Discerning the Real: From the Lam rim chen mo
of Tsôn-kha-pa, tr. Alex Wayman   1978
The Hermit and the Love-Thief: Sanskirt Poems of Bhartrihari and
Bilhaṇa, tr. Barbara Stoler Miller   1978
The Lute: Kao Ming's P'i-p'a chi, tr. Jean Mulligan. Also in
paperback ed.   1980
A Chronicle of Gods and Sovereigns: Jinnō Shōtōki of Kitabatake
Chikafusa, tr. H. Paul Varley.   1980
Among the Flowers: The Hua-chien chi, tr. Lois Fusek   1982
Grass Hill: Poems and Prose by the Japanese Monk Gensei, tr.
Burton Watson   1983
Doctors, Diviners, and Magicians of Ancient China: Biographies of
Fang-shih, tr. Kenneth J. DeWoskin. Also in paperback
ed.   1983
Theater of Memory: The Plays of Kālidāsa, ed. Barbara Stoler
Miller. Also in paperback ed.   1984
The Columbia Book of Chinese Poetry: From Early Times to the

Thirteenth Century, ed. and tr. Burton Watson. Also in
paperback ed.   1984
*Poems of Love and War: From the Eight Anthologies and the Ten
Songs of Classical Tamil*, tr. A. K. Ramanujan. Also in
paperback ed.   1985
The Columbia Book of Later Chinese Poetry, ed. and tr. Jonathan
Chaves. Also in paperback ed.   1986
The Tso Chuan: Selections from China's Oldest Narrative History,
tr. Burton Watson   1989
Selected Writings of Nichiren, ed. Philip B. Yampolsky   1990

STUDIES IN ORIENTAL CULTURE

1. *The Ōnin War: History of Its Origins and Background, with a
   Selective Translation of the Chronicle of Ōnin*, by H. Paul
   Varley   1967
2. *Chinese Government in Ming Times: Seven Studies*, ed. Charles
   O. Hucker   1969
3. *The Actors' Analects (Yakusha Rongo)*, ed. and tr. by Charles
   J. Dunn and Bungō Torigoe   1969
4. *Self and Society in Ming Thought*, by Wm. Theodore de
   Bary and the Conference on Ming Thought. Also in
   paperback ed.   1970
5. *A History of Islamic Philosophy*, by Majid Fakhry, 2d ed.   1983
6. *Phantasies of a Love Thief: The Caurapañcāśikā Attributed to
   Bilhaṇa*, by Barbara Stoler Miller   1971
7. *Iqbal: Poet-Philosopher of Pakistan*, ed. Hafeez Malik   1971
8. *The Golden Tradition: An Anthology of Urdu Poetry*, ed. and
   tr. Ahmed Ali. Also in paperback ed.   1973
9. *Conquerors and Confucians: Aspects of Political Change in Late
   Yüan China*, by John W. Dardess   1973
10. *The Unfolding of Neo-Confucianism*, by Wm. Theodore de
    Bary and the Conference on Seventeenth-Century
    Chinese Thought. Also in paperback ed.   1975
11. *To Acquire Wisdom: The Way of Wang Yang-ming*, by Julia
    Ching   1976
12. *Gods, Priests, and Warriors: The Bhṛgus of the Mahābhārata*,
    by Robert P. Goldman   1977
13. *Mei Yao-ch'en and the Development of Early Sung Poetry*, by
    Jonathan Chaves   1976
14. *The Legend of Semimaru, Blind Musician of Japan*, by Susan
    Matisoff   1977
15. *Sir Sayyid Ahmad Khan and Muslim Modernization in India
    and Pakistan*, by Hafeez Malik   1980
16. *The Khilafat Movement: Religious Symbolism and Political
    Mobilization in India*, by Gail Minault   1982
17. *The World of K'ung Shang-jen: A Man of Letters in Early
    Ch'ing China*, By Richard Strassberg   1983
18. *The Lotus Boat: The Origins of Chinese Tz'u Poetry in T'ang
    Popular Culture*, by Marsha L. Wagner   1984

19. *Expressions of Self in Chinese Literature*, ed. Robert E. Hegel
    and Richard C. Hessney   1985
20. *Songs for the Bride: Women's Voices and Wedding Rites of
    Rural India*, by W. G. Archer, ed., Barbara Stoler Miller
    and Mildred Archer   1986
21. *A Heritage of Kings: One Man's Monarchy in the Confucian
    World*, by JaHyun Kim Haboush   1988

COMPANIONS TO ASIAN STUDIES

Approaches to the Oriental Classics, ed. Wm. Theodore de Bary   1959
Early Chinese Literature, by Burton Watson. Also in paperback
ed.   1962
Approaches to Asian Civilizations, ed. Wm. Theodore de Bary
and Ainslie T. Embree   1964
The Classic Chinese Novel: A Critical Introduction, by C. T. Hsia.
Also in paperback ed.   1968
Chinese Lyricism: Shih Poetry from the Second to the Twelfth Century,
tr. Burton Watson. Also in paperback ed.   1971
A Syllabus of Indian Civilization, by Leonard A. Gordon and
Barbara Stoler Miller   1971
Twentieth-Century Chinese Stories, ed. C. T. Hsia and Joseph S.
M. Lau. Also in paperback ed.   1971
A Syllabus of Chinese Civilization, by J. Mason Gentzler, 2d
ed.   1972
A Syllabus of Japanese Civilization, by H. Paul Varley, 2d ed. 1972
An Introduction to Chinese Civilization, ed. John Meskill, with
the assistance of J. Mason Gentzler   1973
An Introduction to Japanese Civilization, ed. Arthur E. Tiedemann 1974
Ukifune: Love in the Tale of Genji, ed. Andrew Pekarik   1982
The Pleasures of Japanese Literature, by Donald Keene   1988
A Guide to Oriental Classics, ed. Wm. Theodore de Bary and
Ainslie T. Embree; third edition ed. Amy Vladek
Heinrich, 2 vols.   1989

INTRODUCTION TO ORIENTAL CIVILIZATIONS
Wm. Theodore de Bary, Editor

Sources of Japanese Tradition, 1958; paperback ed., 2 vols.,
1964
Sources of Indian Tradition, 1958; paperback ed., 2 vols.,
1964; 2d ed., 1988
Sources of Indian Tradition 1988; 2d ed., 2 vols.
Sources of Chinese Tradition, 1960; paperback ed., 2 vols.,
1964

NEO-CONFUCIAN STUDIES

*Instructions for Practical Living and Other Neo-Confucian Writings
by Wang Yang-ming*, tr. Wing-tsit China   1963

Other Works in Asian Studies Series

Reflections on Things at Hand: The Neo-Confucian Anthology, comp.
Chu Hsi and Lü Tsu-ch'ien, tr. Wing-tsit Chan   1967
Self and Society in Ming Thought. by Wm. Theodore de Bary
and the Conference on Ming Thought: Also in paperback
ed.   1970
The Unfolding of Neo-Confucianism, by Wm. Theodore de Bary
and the Conference on Seventeenth-Century Chinese
Thought. Also in paperback ed.   1975
*Principle and Practicality: Essays in Neo-Confucianism and Practical
Learning,* ed. Wm. Theodore de Bary and Irene Bloom.
Also in paperback ed.   1979
The Syncretic Religion of Lin Chao-en, by Judith A. Berling   1980
*The Renewal of Buddhism in China: Chu-hung and the Late Ming
Synthesis,* by Chün-fang Yü   1981
Neo-Confucian Orthodoxy and the Learning of the Mind-and-Heart,
by Wm. Theodore de Bary   1981
Yüan Thought: Chinese Thought and Religion Under the Mongols,
ed. Hok-lam Chan and Wm. Theodore de Bary   1982
The Liberal Tradition in China, by Wm. Theodore de Bary   1983
The Development and Decline of Chinese Cosmology, by John B.
Henderson   1984
The Rise of Neo-Confucianism in Korea, by Wm. Theodore de
Bary and JaHyun Kim Haboush   1985
Chiao Hung and the Restructuring of Neo-Confucianism in Late Ming,
by Edward T. Ch'ien   1985
Neo-Confucian Terms Explained: Pei-hsi tzu-i, by Ch'en Ch'un,
ed. and trans. Wing-tsit Chan   1986
Knowledge Painfully Acquired: K'un-chih chi, by Lo Ch'in-shun,
ed. and trans. Irene Bloom   1987
To Become a Sage: The Ten Diagrams on Sage Learning, by Yi
T'oegye, ed. and trans. Michael C. Kalton   1988
The Message of the Mind in Neo-Confucian Thought, by Wm.
Theodore de Bary   1989

MODERN ASIAN LITERATURE SERIES

Modern Japanese Drama: An Anthology, ed. and tr. Ted Takaya.
Also in paperback ed.   1979
Mask and Sword: Two Plays for the Contemporary Japanese Theater,
Yamazaki Masakazu, tr. J. Thomas Rimer   1980
Yokomitsu Riichi, Modernist, Dennis Keene   1980
Nepali Visions, Nepali Dreams: The Poetry of Laxmiprasad Devkota,
tr. David Rubin   1980
Literature of the Hundred Flowers, vol. 1: Criticism and Polemics,
ed. Hualing Nieh   1981
Literature of the Hundred Flowers, vol. 2: Poetry and Fiction, ed.
Hualing Nieh   1981
Modern Chinese Stories and Novellas, 1919–1949, ed. Joseph S.
M. Lau, C. T. Hsia, and Leo Ou-fan Lee. Also in
paperback ed.   1984

Other Works in Asian Studies Series

A View of the Sea, by Yasuoka Shōtarō, tr. Kären Wigen
Lewis   1984
*Other Worlds; Arishima Takeo and the Bounds of Modern Japanese
Fiction,* by Paul Anderer   1984
Selected Poems of Sŏ Chŏngju, tr. with intro. by David R.
McCann   1989
The Sting of Life: Four Contemporary Japanese Novelists, by Van
C. Gessel   1989
Stories of Osaka Life, by Oda Sakunosuke, tr. Burton Watson   1990